The Tinsleys

Book Five of The Drugstore Series

ALSO BY SD SHELTON

Me, the Crazy Woman, and Breast Cancer

The Drugstore

The Life of Old Pete
Book Two of The Drugstore Series

Talking to Tubby
Book Three of The Drugstore Series

STARRING DOLL DAHL
Book Four of The Drugstore Series

The Tinsleys

Book Five of The Drugstore Series

A Novel
by

SD SHELTON

ENLIGHTEN PRESS

A DIVISION OF ENLIGHTEN COMMUNICATIONS, INC.

Enlighten Press

A Division of Enlighten Communications, Inc.
Norman, Oklahoma

The Tinsleys
Book Five of The Drugstore Series

First Enlighten Press trade paperback edition March 2019

Manufactured in the United States of America

10 9 8 7 6 5 4 3 2 1

Paperback ISBN 978-0-9997297-3-1
EBook ISBN 978-0-9997297-2-4

Library of Congress Control Number: 2018960132

For more information about special discounts for bulk purchases, please contact Enlighten Press at enlightenpress@cox.net

For my lifelong friends,

Monica Boren Klima, Dirk Lucas, Jeff Engemann,

Frankie Wilson, Jr., Stephanie Walker Holt,

and Laura Ingram,

With whom I've been sharing

Great and comical adventures

Since we were kids.

"The bird a nest,

the spider a web,

man friendship."

– William Blake

Chapter One

Long John awoke to the "erring" whispering of Trucker in his ear. He sat up and looked at his diminutive friend.

"Err. Err errr errrr err err," Trucker whispered.

Long John nodded his head and swung his feet over the side of his rickety wooden bed.

"Err err errrr err," Trucker admonished his best friend.

"Okie dokie, I'll hurry" Long John replied.

Long John stood up, and stretched his long lean body, dwarfing Trucker's pudgy little frame. He looked toward the window. There was no sign of light. Then he glanced at the old metal windup alarm clock on his bedside table. The glow in the dark hands were pointing to two a.m.

Long John was used to the middle of the night escapades under the direction of Trucker. It was clear they were about to embark on another.

"Where we a goin'?" he asked the shadowy figure in front of him.

Trucker erred.

"Baseball fields en Jumper Crick fer a swim?"

"Err," Trucker answered.

Both Long John and Trucker were just two of the thirty something residents of Tinsley's Nursing Home in Konawa, (pronounced Con-uh-wa), Oklahoma. Although pegged as a Nursing Home, most of Tinsley's residents were not elderly, but instead, mentally handicapped.

Long John and Trucker had been friends for as long as both could remember. Trucker had been put into the home first, back in 1956. Before that, he had lived in a mental institution in Vinita, Oklahoma. However, because the hospital needed more room, the doctors there decided that his disabilities were not as serious as most of the other patients, and they asked the state for permission to move the little man to Konawa.

Trucker never knew his family because they had institutionalized him by the time he was two. The only family he claimed was Long John, and sometimes if he was in a good mood, the four other residents he allowed to participate in the late night escapes.

Long John, who was aptly named because he was at least six feet tall and skinny as a rail, got to Tinsley's in 1958. He too had come from Vinita, under the same circumstances as Trucker. When Trucker saw him come through the door, it was the only time in his life he had cried.

Trucker had not been fitting into Tinsley's well. No one could understand his erring, and he found it beyond irritating. The frustration he felt at not being able to communicate with the staff or the other residents, made him angrier than he normally was. That was saying a lot, because Trucker most definitely had anger issues. The little Tinsley—as the town's people called the home's residents—had no tolerance for anyone who wanted to stand in the way of him doing whatever he wanted to do.

Long John had always been able to understand Trucker, and had acted as his mouthpiece. If Trucker wanted more fried chicken at dinner, it was Long John who asked for it. If

Trucker thought the new state provided underwear was too scratchy, it was Long John who complained for him. The best part about Long John—as far as Trucker was concerned—was that his friend never minded listening to him. In fact, Long John had been the only person he'd known who had ever seemed to care about what he had to say— and Trucker had a lot to say.

"Err,"

Trucker poked Long John, hoping to speed him up a little. Long John nodded that he would oblige. Then the two tiptoed out of their shared room, and across the hall to Daphney and Lorelei's room.

"Err er," Trucker whispered while shoving Daphney's arm.

"Trucker says git up," Long John poked Lorelei.

She quickly pulled her dumpling like frame straight up in her bed, and blinked. Daphney hadn't moved so Trucker poked her again. This time, he received a moan in response. Lorelei got out of bed and scurried the three feet to Daphney's bed before poking her too.

"Daphney get up." She put her face two inches from her thin roommate's. "Wake up, wake up, wake up."

Lorelei stared intensely at Daphney's face, waiting for her to respond. When Daphney rolled away from her, she took the woman's arm and lifted it up and then let it drop, dead weight, back onto the bed. Daphney still didn't wake.

"Errrrrrrrrrrr," Trucker growled.

Long John took over.

"We'rea gonna leave yas here iffin yas don't git up."

Lorelei stood up on Daphney's bed. She began jumping up and down.

"Get up Daphney. I wanna go with everyone to Jumper Creek and you need to go too." She kicked at her roommate.

Daphney rolled her tiny body over and halfway peeled her eyes open. Lorelei silently clapped her hands.

"Let's go Daphney," she whispered. "We're goin' on a great adventure."

She reached down and pulled Daphney to a sitting position. Then she jumped down and found their shoes.

"Put these on."

She handed her friend a pair of brown moccasin type house shoes and then she sat down and put on her own.

As soon as the two women were done, Trucker motioned for them to follow him. The four residents snuck down the hall, passing two more rooms, before stealthily slipping into Ponder and his roommate's room.

Daphney and Lorelei waited at the door, keeping watch for anyone from the night shift, while Trucker and Long John crept to the side of Ponder's bed and nudged him.

"Err er," Trucker quietly muttered.

"Git up," Long John translated.

Ponder, a bear of a black man, with gray stubble caking his face, opened one eye and peered out at the two faces above him.

"Err er," Trucker repeated.

Ponder got up, went to a small brown wardrobe, and found his shoes. He slipped them on, then turned to the two men.

"Where…we…goin'?"

Ponder had never been one to show any kind of emotion and it was never more clear than in his monotone voice. That, along with the fact that he spoke slower than molasses thickened with cornstarch, made his verbiage almost as annoying as Trucker's undecipherable erring.

"Errrr er err errr errrrr er errrr," Trucker answered.

"We'rea goin' ta tha baseball field en Jumper Crick," Long John submitted.

Ponder's face never changed its stoic disposition.

"Um hm,…fun."

Trucker motioned for Daphney and Lorelei to move out of the way and then gestured for Long John and Ponder to follow him. The small group continued to sneak down the hall, getting closer to the nurses' station.

The band stopped a few feet from the large partition, then stuck their heads around the corner to see if it was manned. Big Joe, an unkempt nurse's aide, had his legs propped up on the white laminate desk. His head was buried in a comic book.

Trucker whispered to Long John who relayed his message.

"Lorelei, Trucker says ta crawl past 'em en go git Maybelline."

Lorelei nodded and set off to find her tall, almost Amazonian friend. The other four backed away from the station, as they watched Lorelei slowly crawl into the darkness of the corridor beyond. It wasn't long before they saw one medium, and one large, shadow crawling back.

Once the two women were safely past the nurse's aide—who remained oblivious to their movements—the group retreated back toward Trucker and Long John's room at end of the hall. Their room sat adjacent to the hall's emergency exit, which had accidently become their portal to freedom.

Several years back, Trucker and Stubby Watts had been fighting in the hallway. Stubby kept going to the doorway of Trucker and Long John's room and showing them his belly. Trucker abhorred seeing Stubby's belly.

Stubby would stand silently at the room's entrance, until either of the roommates noticed his presence. As soon as one did, he would raise his shirt up to his neck, stick his pasty white belly out, and grin like a Cheshire Cat.

Although Long John rarely, if ever, paid him any attention, it infuriated Trucker to no end.

"Errrrr err err er errr!!!" Trucker would yell to the thirty-something year old boy man.

"He says ta git outta here," Long John would disclose.

Stubby would squint, then clinch his teeth together and raise his lips, revealing his yellowed, and sometimes Cheetos caked, dentures. Then, he would run away as fast as he could.

One day, when Trucker had been in an exceptionally foul mood, Stubby made the mistake of showing his belly one time too many.

The moment Stubby pulled up his shirt, Trucker lunged from his bed, and tore into the crusty Tinsley. The two wrestled up and down the hall until Trucker managed to throw Stubby into the exit door, sending him sprawling outside onto the grass.

Trucker waited for the alarm to alert the staff that an escape route had been breached, but it never sounded. Trucker looked around to make sure no one had seen the commotion, and upon realizing they hadn't, he rushed to the door.

He pushed Stubby—who was still sprawled on the ground—out of the way and quickly closed the door. Then he opened it again, and waited for the alarm. The silence remained. Still unbelieving of his good fortune, Trucker closed the door one last time before reopening it. It was dead quiet.

Trucker looked behind him to ensure he was still free from prying eyes, and when he realized he was, he did a happy dance. He swirled in circles, grinning to show every tiny little tooth in his head, all the while, erring nonstop to the empty hall around him.

That very night, he rounded up the other five residents, and began, what would become the first of many, late night adventures.

Chapter Two

Trucker, whose real name was Harold, had gotten his nickname shortly after he got to Tinsleys. Although no one knew why, he had a serious obsession for pickup trucks.

Unlike in most towns, the Tinsleys were allowed to roam the streets of their own free will. Because of his freedom, Trucker had unlimited occasions to throw himself fully into his fetish.

The first time it happened, the townsfolk thought it was a fluke. However, it turned out that his odd behavior had continued throughout the twenty-some years of his stay, becoming an accepted part—and hazard—of driving a pickup truck. Trucker intrusions became as much a part of the town as the churches on almost every corner.

On his first outing from the nursing home, he had walked the quarter of a mile into town where he found a wonderful 1944 Ford truck parked at Harvey's Gas Station. The truck was like an irresistible magnet to the dwarfish man. The dark blue oxidized vehicle beckoned to him to take a ride, so he jumped up in the bed, and sat on the wheel well waiting for its owner to fulfill his wish.

When Babe Honeycutt finished paying for his gasoline, and emerged from the small office in front of the station, he saw Trucker perched in back. He had no idea who the man was or why he was in the truck, so he circled the bed to get a better look.

"Can I help you?" he curiously asked the Tinsley.

"Err er er errr." Trucker smiled, showing several empty spaces where teeth used to reside.

Mr. Honeycutt looked around to see if there was anyone who could translate.

Henry Fisher, the gas station attendant, was standing inside the open garage with his back to the scene. Babe hollered at him.

"Henry, can ya come here?"

Henry rounded the front of the vehicle and sauntered past the driver's side door before looking to where Mr. Honeycutt was pointing.

"You know who this is?" Babe asked him.

"Nope, never seen em," Henry answered.

"Hey buddy, whatcha doing back there?" Babe asked Trucker.

"Errr er errr," Trucker answered.

Both men looked at each other to see if either had understood the answer. Neither had.

"You go on now; get outta my truck," Babe tried to shoo the man away.

Trucker remained seated. Babe and Henry looked at one another again, both unsure of how they should proceed.

"Git now," Henry pointed down the road, attempting to get Trucker to exit the bed.

Trucker remained seated.

"I bet he's one of them there Tinsleys," Henry finally deduced.

"Ohhhh," Babe nodded in agreement, "Well that's just a fine how do ya do," he flatly stated. "Wadda you think we should do?" He turned to look at the attendant.

"Beats me," Henry shrugged. I guess I can git the broom and git em out."

Babe nodded again. "Yep, I think that's the thing to do."

Babe continued to watch Trucker, who seemed irritated.

"Err er," Trucker spit. "Err!" He motioned for Babe to get in the cab.

"I ain't takin' you with me," Babe responded, as if he had understood the little man. "You need to get outta my truck."

"Er," Trucker responded, still refusing to move.

Henry appeared with the broom, and handed it to Babe. Babe looked at him, surprised.

"I ain't gettin' him out." He shook his head. "You do it." He handed the broom back to Henry.

Henry let out a big sigh before stepping closer to the truck.

"This is your last chance," he told Trucker. "Git outta the truck now or you're gonna be sorry."

Trucker remained seated, clearly more irritated than ever, and let out a strand of what seemed to be dirty curse words, although none of them were intelligible.

"I don't think he's gonna budge." Henry looked at Babe.

"Nope, don't think he is," Babe agreed.

Both men continued to stare at Trucker, sizing up the Tinsley, and their chances of sweeping him out. Finally Henry sighed and lifted the broom. Trucker, realizing that instead of a ride, he was going to get swatted, stood up, let out another torrent of errs and climbed out over the tailgate. When he reached the ground he turned to the two and spit at their feet. Then he walked off, looking back every few feet to err at them some more.

Both Babe and Henry stood motionless for several moments, watching the Tinsley walk away muttering erring profanities to himself.

Babe eventually turned to Henry. "Well, I guess I'll see ya next time."

"Okay then," Henry responded. "See ya next time."

When Trucker attempted to get a ride a couple of days later, word spread quickly about him, and his love of trucks. That time it was Boomer Daw's fifty-two Chevy that Trucker had fixated upon.

Boomer had been parked in front of the western wear store. When he came out, he saw Trucker exactly as he had been in Babe Honeycutt's truck, on the wheel well, acting like it was the most natural thing in the world.

Much as before, Boomer asked the man what he was doing in his truck, to which Trucker erred an undecipherable reply. Boomer tried to coax him from the bed, but Trucker kept pointing for him to get in the cab. It wasn't difficult for Boomer to realize Trucker wanted a ride, but he wasn't about to give it to him. He had no idea who Trucker was, or worse, if he was dangerous.

Mariah Roberts, the owner of the Western Wear Store, saw Boomer by the side of his truck, wildly gesturing to the bed. Her curiosity got the best of her and she went outside to see what was happening.

"This here un's in my truck and won't get out," Boomer informed her.

Mariah looked the burr headed and pock marked Tinsley up and down before revealing his identity.

"That there is a Tinsley." She turned to Boomer. "Be careful of 'em. Sometimes don't know how they're gonna react."

"Ohhhh," Boomer nodded his understanding. "Well that makes sense. He must be a new one. Haven't seen him 'round here before."

"Why's he in your truck?" Mariah squinted at Trucker, who erred at her.

"Don't reckon I know." Boomer shrugged. "Maybe he wants a ride?"

With that declaration Trucker stood up, and jumped up and down, while erring at the two. Then he motioned again for Boomer to get in the cab.

"Yep, that what he wants all right," Mariah conceded.

"Well I ain't got time for that nonsense," Boomer responded as he turned back to Trucker.

"You gonna have to get out cause I ain't got time for that."

Trucker stomped his foot, and furiously shook his head no.

"Now you've gone and upset em," Mariah observed. "That's never a good thing ya know."

"I don't care. Hannah is waitin' for me so I can take her to Maiden to get some cake decoratin' supplies. I gotta get out of here."

Trucker had ceased with his foot stomping and was instead eyeing Boomer to see if he was going to change his mind.

Boomer raised his voice, which is actually what got him the nickname Boomer.

"I done told ya to get your butt outta my pickup truck!"

The very loud and forceful declaration startled Trucker into abandoning his sit in. Now a little scared, Trucker wouldn't look at Boomer as he departed.

As soon as he was out, he regained his courage, and turned to spit at the burly man. He stopped cold in his tracks before he did. Seeing him from street view instead of pickup bed view, he realized the man was gargantuan in comparison to himself. He turned and ran off.

Some of the menfolk had declared that if it wasn't for Ike Stephens giving Trucker a ride a week later, they could have all avoided the last twenty years of Trucker's truck bed fiascos.

Ike, after exiting the Eater Upper, found Trucker in the back of his clover green Studebaker. He examined the pudgy interloper for only second before he nonchalantly issued an invitation.

"Ya need a ride there son?" Ike asked.

With a monstrous looking grin, Trucker displayed every one of his remaining yellow baby looking teeth.

"Well okay then," Ike said while getting into the cab, "but, hang on; don't want ya flyin' out round the curves."

Before leaving the parking lot, Ike leaned out the window and looked back at his passenger. "Where ya goin?"

Trucker pointed to the old highway which led north, out of town, and conveniently past Tinsley's.

"Goin' that way myself, so no trouble."

Ike started the engine and pulled out of the gravel lot.

As the two drove away, Trucker was grinning bigger than a crocodile at an all-you-can-eat buffet.

Chapter Three

That first night, the six pajama clad Tinsleys exited the nursing home onto the brown and dry grass outside the door. The moon was half full, providing just enough light for them to easily cross the lawn and reach the one lane street behind the home.

Lorelei skipped ahead of the rest as they made their way to North Street—the main cross street. It led past a few small houses, the County Barn, and the public swimming pool, before it met up with State Street, which circled the city park.

When they made it to the park, the group opted to cut through it instead of staying on the road. They crossed a small ravine—which dumped runoff water from Jumper Creek—before finally stopping at the big metal ocean wave merry-go-round.

The merry-go-round wasn't the traditional type that sat on the ground. Instead, it balanced from a tall pole. The construction allowed the merry-go-round to actually swing back and forth as well as circular.

Ponder languidly, and awkwardly, climbed onto a wooden seat. He motioned for the rest of the group to get aboard. Lorelei and Daphney both tried to climb onto the same bench. They struggled between themselves to take claim. Maybelline tried to stop the ensuing war.

"Lorelei, come on this side with me." She patted the seat next to her.

Lorelei looked up from her power struggle, and quickly lost the seat to Daphney, who then stuck her tongue out at her roommate. Lorelei hmphed her displeasure before joining Maybelline on the other side.

Trucker backed away from the contraption. He hated the merry-go-round. He had gotten motion sick on it several years earlier and threw up the roast beef he had had for that night's dinner. He plopped down to the ground, content to watch his friends ride.

"Push…us…Long…John," Ponder's forlorn, and rather sad sounding voice echoed through the night.

"Make go back and forth," Daphney, ordered.

"Yeah," Maybelline agreed.

"Awww, thet ain't no fair." Long John stuck his lower lip out in a pout. "I wanna ride."

"You…can…ride," Ponder assured his friend. "Just…push…us…first…den…I'll…push…us."

Long John smiled a smile which lit up the night.

"Okie dokie," he agreed. "I'll push yas now en yas push later."

Trucker erred his displeasure at having to wait before going to the ball field, but knowing it was in vain, he laid back on the ground and looked up at the many bright stars overhead.

Long John ran as fast as he could, pushing the swinging cage. Then he jumped back to watch it twirl.

"Make us go back en forth," Daphney reiterated.

Long John took a running leap at the swing and shoved it as hard as he could toward the pole. The swing hit the metal pole sending a loud clanking sound through the otherwise still night.

"Errr errr err," Trucker sat up and whispered-yelled to Long John.

"Yeah," Long John agreed. "We'rea gonna wake everyun up."

The group looked up State Street, which was lined with houses. A window on a house three doors up the street illuminated with light, revealing a small silhouette. Everyone hushed, watching the figure in the window, until the light went out and no others appeared.

"We…better…git…outta…here," Ponder said. "Someone …could…be…comin'…to…see…what's…goin'…on."

The Boy Scout Hut and the old armory were located directly after the houses ended on State Street. Trucker pointed to the ball field sat at the end of the road where State Street made a U-turn and became Madison Street again.

"Err err."

"Ballfield," Long John stated.

All six Tinsleys crossed the street over to the armory. As they started to follow a grassy path to the field, Long John pointed to a rather large window on the right front side of the armory.

"Thur's a light en thur."

Each Tinsley turned to follow Long John's finger.

"Let my see," Daphney interjected. "It bright."

"It's a weird color," Maybelline noted. "Gray."

Everyone forgot their mission to get to the field and instead headed toward the otherwise darkened, and somewhat menacing structure.

Trucker was the first to make it to the window. He turned around and looked at the rest of the gathering bewildered.

"Errr er errrr er errr." He shrugged.

Long John pushed him aside, annoying Trucker enough for him to growl at his friend.

"He's right, ain't no light en hurr." He too, turned to the others and shrugged.

Ponder stepped back from the group and looked up.

"It's... up... dere." He pointed to the top pane in the group of twelve.

Everyone stepped back and looked at the window again. Then they gasped in unison.

"It move," Daphney put her hand to her cheek.

"That's neato," Lorelei giggled. "It moves!"

"It...kinda...looks...like...da...moon." Ponder tilted his head, while examining the gray light.

"Hey that is the moon!" Maybelline turned around to face them. "It's just a flection—like in the mirror."

Then she snorted and grabbed her stomach.

"Ya'll is silly. "Ya'll thought that flection was a light."

Trucker scowled at her.

"It ain't funny Maybelline," Lorelei chastised. "You thought it was a light too."

"Did not." Maybelline shook her head in denial.

"Did too!" Lorelei argued.

"Did not neither." Maybelline jutted out her chin.

"Did too! Did too! Did too!"

Long John stepped between the two feuding women and sighed.

"Its don't matter." He shrugged his shoulders. "We's gonna stand here en argue all night or we's gonna have fun?"

Lorelei reluctantly huffed, while Maybelline turned to look back at the building.

"Hey, maybe we can get in."

She took off for the north side of the tall red brick, and concrete formed façade. Only a moment after she disappeared, she called to the rest of them.

"Hurry you guys! Come here!"

Ponder was the last of the group to round the corner, and he saw Long John jumping underneath another multi-paned but high window. Although he was tall, he could barely see into the darkness that engulfed the building's interior.

"Lift me; I wanna see," Lorelei ordered.

"I kin't," Long John informed the somewhat hefty woman. "Ya's too big fer me."

Lorelei sulked at Long John's pronouncement.

"Let my see," Daphney said to Ponder. "Lift."

Ponder looked down at her. She was barely five feet and thin as a rail. He heaved her over his head and turned her to face the window.

"See nothing." She looked down at the others.

"Wish we cud git en thur," Long John said.

The others agreed.

"Let's go to the other side," Maybelline ordered them.

When they got there, they found two very large white garage doors. Maybelline had an idea that she remembered from watching the Super Friends cartoons, that morning.

"You guys watch me," she boasted, while motioning for her friends to gather around the farthest door. "I am Wonder Woman. I am so strong that I will lift this door over my head," she declared. Then she bent down to grab the handle in the center of it.

"You...ain't...gonna...be...able...ta...lift...it," Ponder sluggishly interjected. "It'll...be...locked...," he was not able to finish his sentence before the door slid up about two feet.

Everyone gasped, except Ponder who remained unfazed.

"Err." Trucker's eyes lit up.

"Itsa's open." Long John tilted his head in wonderment.

"Let's go!" Lorelei jumped in front of them all, and forced her hefty bum under the door, and into the darkness.

The rest followed with ease, except for Ponder and Maybelline. Each had to be pulled through the narrow space. Although Maybelline huffed and snorted as the others tugged at her, Ponder silently acquiesced, while the group forced his beefy frame inside.

From the moon cascading through the windows, shadowy outlines of a couple of trucks could be seen. A large cylinder stood toward the back of the enormous cavern of the hanger like building. Lorelei took off in that direction. The rest of the group followed her lead, but more hesitantly.

"What if it's haunted," Maybelline asked, remembering the morning's episode of Scooby Doo.

"Err er." Trucker shook his head.

"Yeah," Long John agreed, "its ain't."

"How do you know?" she haughtily challenged. "You don't know everything Trucker." She put her hands on her hips and glared down at the miniscule man.

"Errr," Trucker growled back at her.

Daphney grabbed ahold of the back of Maybelline's pajama top, fearing too, that the old building may house a ghost or two.

"I not go," she shivered. "Ghosties."

"See I told you there was ghostises. She said it was true!" Maybelline pointed to Daphney, then she sneered at Trucker, who sneered back.

"There ain't no ghostises," Lorelei turned to the two other women. "See I's here and nothin' got me." She threw her arms out to her side and spun around to show them she was okay.

The men eagerly followed Lorelei further inside—Long John running toward the parked vehicles. He went to the first one, which had a flat bed. He sprang up on the step and opened the cab door before hopping in behind the steering wheel. He immediately began moving the wheel back and forth causing the tires to slightly screech on the heavily polished concrete floor.

"Look ya'll; Imma drivin'!" He grinned.

The rest of the group made a beeline to the vehicle. Trucker sprang into the bed before the rest had time to move.

Ponder staked his claim in the passenger seat, while the girls joined Trucker in the back.

"Hold on tight cuz we gonna go extra, super, dooper, fast—faster en lightnin'," Long John declared.

Trucker erred his pleasure, and the girls squealed in terror.

"Ya ready?" Long John looked back at his cargo. They nodded yes.

"Ya ready Ponder?" he looked to his sidekick.

"Yessem," Ponder stalled as if it took great effort to release his words. "Imma... ready."

Long John made an engine noise with his mouth which got louder with every second.

"Hang on!" Long John yelled, as he took the wheel and shoved it to the right as far as it would go. He leaned into the "turn" with his whole body like he was being thrown from the force. Ponder sat motionless until Long John nudged him.

"Hey, yas gotta lean like me when we goes round tha corners," he ordered.

Ponder, wordless, stared back at him.

Long John turned to the bunch behind him. "Yas gotta lean like me when we's goes round tha corners."

"Ohhhh," Daphney acknowledged.

Long John then swung the wheel to the left, his body rolling with it. Trucker and the girls did the same, but again, Ponder sat upright, and motionless.

Just as Long John was getting ready to admonish him, Ponder rolled to the left. In usual Ponder fashion, he was just slower than the rest.

The group continued the speedy and curvaceous "ride." The girls squealed with every turn, and Trucker grinned from ear to ear. Ponder remained impassive, continuing his late leaning each time, sometimes remaining to one side long after the rest of the group had already taken another curve in the opposite direction. Long John became a little agitated by it, but didn't say any more.

Maybelline soon tired of the driving game and stood up in the bed, surveying all that lay in the darkness.

"Let's go look around."

"Awww," Long John sulked. "I wasa havin' fun."

He remained behind the steering wheel waiting for his comrades to agree with him. When they didn't, he reluctantly released the wheel and climbed down the large truck.

The rest of the group, with the exception of Ponder, climbed down too. Ponder, still in a lean from the last curve, remained in the cab a few more moments before he too descended.

"What that?" Daphney pointed to a large wooden door perched atop a narrow flight of stairs on the far end of the building.

"Let's open that door too." Maybelline grinned.

"Ghosties," Daphney whispered again, while moving to hide behind Lorelei.

"There ain't no ghostises Daphney. Stop bein' a big ole baby," Lorelei scoffed.

Daphney's head began to lower and her lip began to quiver with her hurt feelings.

"I no baby," she pouted.

"Come on." Maybelline ignored Daphney and waved the others to follow her.

She and Lorelei marched toward the door before turning to make sure their cohorts were at hand. The little line of Tinsleys slunk across the armory floor, each looking around them for any signs of life or death. When they got to the base of the stairs Ponder halted the group.

"One...two...free...fo...five...six...sebun."

The assembly turned to look at Ponder who was slowly, and methodically, counting each stair.

"Sebun. There...are...sebun." He looked at his friends as if they should know how important it was.

The gang blankly returned his stare.

"Sebun..."   he   slowly   stated   again. "So's...we...can...go... up...Daphney. Dere's...sebun."

For whatever reason, Ponder's assertion that they could proceed because there were seven stairs was enough to make Daphney more comfortable, and she nodded.

"No ghosties," she whispered.

Trucker was becoming impatient. He pushed Lorelei to the side, stepped in front of Maybelline, and began ascending the stairs. When he got to the top one, he leaned against the door to listen to whatever may be on the other side. Seemingly, he felt it was safe, because he put his hand on the old metal and somewhat rusty doorknob and turned it.

Everyone below him gasped, which aggravated Trucker so he turned to err at them. When they all lowered their heads from the scolding, he then turned back to the doorway to peer inside.

"Watcha… see?" Ponder listlessly inquired.

"Errerr."

"Nuttin?" Long John questioned.

Trucker opened the door a little wider, and the group repeated their earlier gasp. Trucker jumped, scared from their outburst.

"Err err!" he admonished them.

"Sorry," Long John apologized, before heading up the stairs himself. The rest followed.

"Err er errr." Trucker turned to Long John.

Long John pressed his unusually long neck through the doorway. "Yep, itsa desk," he agreed.

"I wanna see."

Maybelline took her stout frame and pushed Lorelei and Daphney aside. She lumbered up the rest of the steps before pushing Long John and Trucker aside too.

"Um hm, there's a desk," she concurred.

The rest of the group hit the top of the stairs and blew through the door to stare at the desk.

"Whose desk is it?" Lorelei questioned.

"Maybe...da...president's." Ponder stood expressionless, looking at the workspace.

"Who present?" Daphney asked Maybelline.

She shrugged, not knowing.

"Who present?" Daphney then asked Lorelei.

Lorelei looked at Long John who shrugged too.

"Who present?" she finally asked Ponder.

"He...dat...man...dat's...on...da...TV," Ponder replied. "He... gots...a...big...ole...desk."

"Is present's!" Daphney squealed, and ran to sit in the seat behind it. "I on TV." She smiled as she began to twirl around in the chair.

Trucker paid no mind to Daphney and instead began looking around the small office. He saw two flags in the corner. One looked to be blue and one looked like it was stripped. He thought he had seen it before on firecracker day at the park.

"Errrrr," he said to Long John.

"Ohhhhh." Long John's eyes got as round as saucers. "Where?" He turned to the others.

"He says thur's firecrackers!"

"Where?" Lorelei demanded. "I want firecrackers."

"I want firecrackers too." Maybelline nodded.

"Firecrackers." Daphney stopped her whirling to whisper.

"Where...are...da...firecrackers?" Ponder asked Long John, who looked at Trucker.

Trucker pointed to the desk. Everyone ran toward it, pushing Daphney and her chair to the back wall.

Lorelei opened the top center drawer and found some pencils. Ponder was trying to open the bottom right drawer, but it wasn't budging. Trucker and Long John worked on the two left drawers. Long John pulled out a yellow lined note pad and Trucker pulled out a framed document which he held up for all to see.

"Errrrrrrrrrr," he said, very enamored.

"What is its?"

Long John tried to take the frame from his friend. Trucker pulled it back and clutched it tightly to his chest. Then he turned away from the group as if protecting an invaluable artifact.

"Let us see!" Maybelline protested and stamped her foot.

"Yeah!" The rest of the troop said in unison.

Trucker eyed them suspiciously, as if none of them could be trusted. Then he backed away, still holding the frame closely. When he made it a safe distance, he held up the artifact to inspect it.

"Errr errr errr err er." He held his chin in the air as if he were royalty.

"Wadda…he…say…Long…John?" Ponder queried.

"He said itsa from tha president," Long John reported.

"Ohhhhh," replied the group, collectively.

"Wad...is...it?" Ponder monotonously questioned his friend.

Trucker erred.

"It's portant," Long John told the others before turning to Trucker. "Kin I see it?"

Trucker eyed him long and hard, but then decided it was safe to share with his friend. He handed it to Long John. The frame held an official looking document.

"What it?" Daphney asked him.

"Itsa too dark fer me ta see," Long John replied.

"Go to the window," Lorelei pointed to the sole window located at the side of the desk, which had a streak of the street lamp flowing through it.

Long John complied.

"It says 'Dis here is tha president's desk," he pretended to read. "Only tha president kin sit here."

He looked straight at Daphney who immediately disagreed.

"No, I sit," she pointed to herself sitting in the chair.

"Uh uh," Lorelei argued, "it says only the president can sit there." She put her hands on her hips.

"I sit," Daphney again protested.

"I don't think itsa good idea fer ya ta sit thur Daphney," Long John interjected. "Ya may git en trouble."

Daphney exhaled loudly, resigning herself to the idea of giving up her chair.

"I not sit," she stood up.

"Let's go back out there," Maybelline, pointed to the door. "Let's see if there's more president stuff."

She led them all out the door. Daphney stalled and looked back, still upset that she wasn't allowed in the present's chair.

Chapter Four

D aphney was twenty-six. Her mother, who had given birth to her late in life, had passed away just two years previously. Her father had died when Daphney was only two, and she had no memory of him.

Daphney had only one sibling—a much older sister named Susie, who had already been in her twenties when Daphney was born. When the girls' mother got ill and could no longer take care of Daphney, Susie took the elderly woman into her own home and moved Daphney into Tinsley's.

"It's only for a little while, until I get mother well" she told Daphney. "I'm sorry, I can't take care of you both."

Susie cried when she was helping her sister settle into her new room. Daphney patted her sister's shoulder.

"It okay Sissy," she tried to console her. "I be okay."

"Mom and I will visit every day," her sister promised.

Daphney clapped her hands and smiled.

For several weeks, her mother and sister did visit every day and Daphney enjoyed it. But it wasn't long before she made friends with other residents (something she never had before), and she wanted to play more than she wanted to visit. In fact, most days, she would only stop her playing long enough to hug the two women hello before she would run off to be with her pals.

So for the rest of her stay, until her mother got too ill to come, her sister changed their visitations to Sundays when they would have lunch with her.

Daphney's mousy brown hair had already begun to show premature streaks of gray, but her hazel-green eyes remained bright and childlike. She had a diminutive stature that allowed her to hide behind others when shyness struck her, which was often.

She had become best friends with Lorelei, more out of necessity, than a need for companionship. Lorelei was boisterous and not afraid of anything. Daphney used her roommate as a human shield, and a mouthpiece the majority of their time together.

Before the facility made them roommates, Daphney shared her room with a woman named Betty. Betty was more or less confined to her bed. She was unable to speak or even move on her own—her body crippled with contractures caused by Muscular Dystrophy.

Daphney felt helpless and alone while paired with the invalid. She also became depressed, having to watch the woman's anguish, as she moaned and writhed in pain.

Daphney had never confessed it to anyone, but she was glad when Betty finally died of a heart attack. She didn't think it was right that anyone should have to suffer that much.

It wasn't long before Lorelei was moved into her room.

The brazen girl hadn't really stopped talking since that day, but her incessant chatter was a comfort to Daphney because it kept her from having to speak.

It was also okay with Daphney that Lorelei had Down's syndrome, because it meant the two had something in common. She was the first person that Daphney had felt normal around.

Best of all, Daphney didn't have to watch anyone else suffer.

At first, Daphney wasn't thrilled with her new roommate, especially after she had taken her prized possession. It was a brown porcelain dog that Daphney's mother had given her when her own dog, Brownie, had died.

Telling her new roommate that it was so cute that it should be placed where they both could see it, Lorelei took the dog and moved it from Daphney's dresser to a large armoire on the wall facing their beds.

Daphney watched in horror as Lorelei grabbed the figurine, then marched over to the piece of furniture. Lorelei fumbled with it until she finally got it to stand up. She turned to Daphney, a proud smile overtaking her face.

Daphney wasn't smiling at all, because she believed that, after his death, Brownie had moved inside the figurine and she talked to it daily. She glared at Lorelei, but was too shy to voice her displeasure. Instead, she waited until Lorelei left the room and she moved the dog back, telling him that it was going to be okay and that she would protect him. When

Lorelei returned and saw Daphney talking to the dog, she too became upset.

"Why did you move our dog?"

Daphney hugged the dog closer to her and starred at Lorelei without saying a word. Lorelei tried to take the dog from Daphney, but the diminutive girl mustered her courage. She flung her body to the side, blocking Lorelei and yelled at the interloper.

"No, mine!"

Lorelei jumped back and stared at Daphney.

"We need to share the doggie," she asserted. "It's pretty. He can be ours together."

"No mine," Daphney now whispered, continuing to clutch the dog close to her chest.

Lorelei hmphed but gave up the fight easily.

"Let's go play." She jumped up and down with excitement.

Daphney eyed her suspiciously. After sizing her up a few moments, and coming to the conclusion that having another person to play with was worth the risk of setting down the dog, she did just that, and the two ran off together. They had been inseparable ever since.

Daphney missed her mother a lot. When she first passed away, Daphney cried constantly. She had only seen her mother twice during the month she had departed. Both times, Susie had taken her from Tinsleys, and brought her to their mother's bedside. She remembered when Susie came to the home on a Wednesday—leaving Daphney confused, because she had already eaten lunch with Lorelei and didn't want to eat again.

"I'm not here for lunch," Susie told her, as she sat her down on the bed. She took her sister's small hand. "I need to tell you that Momma is gone. She went to Heaven to be with Daddy and Brownie."

Daphney smiled leaving Susie to realize she didn't understand.

"You won't be able to see Momma anymore," she rephrased her earlier attempt. This time, Daphney furrowed her brow.

"I see her. You take," she flatly stated.

"No, I can't because Momma is gone. Just like when Brownie died and you couldn't see him for real anymore. It's like that for Momma. You can see her in your mind, but you won't be able to see her for real. She's gone."

When the news sunk in, it was too much for Daphney to take. She demanded that Susie bring their mother to her right then. She screamed, and threw her pillow at the woman. She stomped her feet, and even cursed.

"My momma!" she yelled. "Mine! Get her! Get her! Get her! Get her!"

Susie tried to comfort and hold her, but Daphney was having none of it. She tore loose from her sister's embrace and continued to scream and cry.

"My momma! My momma! Mine! Bring me! Bring me now!" She wiped her eyes and nose on her sleeve. Then she collapsed as a sobbing heap upon her bed. "My momma," she whispered, "mine."

Susie took Daphney to the funeral. Daphney wouldn't leave the casket. She bent over and whispered for her mother to wake up.

"Up Momma," she sweetly said. "You up."

When her mother didn't move, Daphney touched her cheek, but feeling coldness instead of the warm, rose petal like skin she was used to, her hand recoiled. She turned to her sister, her eyes questioning.

Susie wrapped Daphney in her arms to try and console her, but she wrenched away and leaned over her mother's corpse.

"Up Momma!" she urged the body. "Up Momma!"

Tears began streaming down her face and she grabbed her mother's lifeless arm and tugged. Susie took hold of the grieving woman child and gently pulled her back.

"She's not here anymore." She looked into Daphney's eyes. "She left her body and went to Heaven."

Susie pointed up to the ceiling. Daphney's eyes followed.

"No Heaven," she furrowed her brow. "She here." Daphney pointed to the casket.

"No Baby Doll," Susie called her younger sister by the pet name that her mother had given her.

"I still Momma's Baby Doll?" Daphney searched her sister's eyes.

"You will always be Momma's baby doll," Susie assured her sibling. "Forever, and ever, and ever. And, one day we will get to go be with Momma in Heaven, and she will call you her baby doll again." She patted Daphney's hand.

Finally, Daphney nodded and turned to walk away.

"I Momma's baby doll," she deeply sighed. "I see in Heben."

When Susie tried to move Daphney in with her, Daphney did not want to go. She was settled at the home with Lorelei, and couldn't imagine leaving her best friend. So, Susie allowed her to stay, and she continued her weekly Sunday visits for lunch.

Those first few months, after her mother's departure, Daphney cried herself to sleep every night. She would lie in bed remembering how—when she still lived at home—her mother would come each night and tuck her into bed.

Daphney was about ten when she realized that she was different, especially when the little girl who lived next door had stopped playing with her.

"Why she not play Momma?" Daphney had questioned. "Cause I'm wetarded?"

Daphney saw the horrible pain that crossed her mother's face when she asked the question; but then her mother sat up, held her head high, and set her daughter straight.

"Daphney, it's true that you are retarded, but that isn't a bad thing. In fact it's a wonderful thing." She paused to warmly smile at Daphney.

"I have to tell you that when the doctors first told me that you had Down's syndrome, I cried because I knew it meant that you would be different from everyone else." She closed her eyes remembering that day.

"I thought that you being different was a bad thing, but I was so wrong." She squeezed the child's hand before bringing it up to her lips and kissing it.

"You wrong?" Daphney looked up at the woman that she loved more than anyone.

"Yes Baby Doll, wrong," she answered. "I remember being sad because being retarded means that you will stay a child your whole life—you won't ever grow up. I was crushed thinking that you were going to miss out on so much in life."

Daphney sadly bit her lower lip.

"No, Honey." She lifted her child's chin so she could meet her eyes. "I was seeing it incorrectly, because I realized that the best part of my life—until your sister and you came along—was when I was a child. I played all day. In the summer, I ran in the fields and hunted for bugs, and toads, and butterflies. In the winter, I played in the snow, and built snowmen. I was so happy, with nothing to do but use my imagination, and play. That's when I realized that you are so special, and that God must have loved you more than most." She clasped her daughter's hand to her chest.

"I special?"

"Oh you are," her mother assured her. "See God decided to let you be a child your whole life. Other people have to grow up, and work. They have to take care of a house, and they have difficult responsibilities. They hardly ever get to play." She raised her eyebrows, checking to see if Daphney understood.

"I was sad that you would always be a child, until I realized—you will always get be a child, and that is a wonderful thing! You will never have to grow up and lose all the best of who you are. Yes, God loved you for sure."

Daphney had a huge grin plastered across her face, and she giggled. "I special," she agreed.

"And I'm going to tell you a little secret," her mother leaned closer and whispered.

"Secret," Daphney whispered back.

"There's another reason you are special. I think you and all the children who have Down's are really angels in disguise." Her eyes grew big and she nudged her daughter.

"Angels?" Daphney whispered back, but then shook her head. "I not have wings Momma."

"Oh I know," she giggled, "your wings are invisible."

"How I angel Momma?" Daphney quizzed.

"You are a reminder to everyone else that no matter what their circumstances, they should choose to be happy." She gave Daphney a little tap on her nose.

"What I mean is that I never, ever, see you without a smile on your face. I never see any of your friends that have Down's without a smile. Some of your friends have trouble walking. Some are even in wheelchairs, but they are always happy. You teach the rest of us to live in our joy, because if you all can do it when you have such difficulties, then nobody else has any excuse not to be joyful."

Daphney smiled at her mother again and snuggled into her, smelling her freshly washed hair and the lavender soap her mother used to bathe.

Her mother sighed.

"And that means that God really loved me too, because he sent me my very own beautiful, and special angel," she sighed.

>o<

Daphney would smile at the remembrance of that conversation, until she realized that her mother was gone from her forever. Then the tears would flow.

In the two years that had passed, the tears came less, although she still soaked her pillow a couple of times a week. It was then that Lorelei's presence was invaluable. She would leave her own bed and crawl into Daphney's. There she would hold the girl and rock her back and forth.

"Shhh, Daphney," she'd soothingly say, "it's gonna be okay. I promise."

Then she would tickle her under the arms until Daphney squealed. The two would then snuggle down under the covers and fall asleep in each other's arms.

Chapter Five

The small entourage tumbled down the office steps and back onto the main floor of the armory. Each of them scattered in their own direction, searching for the next exciting thing they could find.

It wasn't long before Trucker erred at them, and they scurried like field mice to another stairway on the opposite side of the building. This one went down instead of up.

"Err," Trucker pointed at the closed door at the bottom of the steps.

"Ohhhh," came a united reply.

Trucker motioned for the group to follow him, and they descended down the stairway. When Trucker got to the door, he turned to look at the rest of them, his eyes wide with fright and excitement.

"I not go." Daphney crossed her arms and shook her head.

"Why?" Lorelei whined. "It'll be fun. I bet this is where the president lives." She excitedly jumped up and down.

Ponder jutted out his chin as if he was trying to remember something important.

"I...don't...knows...'bout...dat." He scratched his head.

"Why?" Long John asked.

"Dis...don't...look...like...dat...house...I...seen...on... da...telebision."

"Hmm. I thinks we shud still take a look en thur." Long John stepped forward but then suddenly stopped.

He turned to the group.

"What if thur is somun in thur? Maybe we ought not ta open it."

"Open it!" Maybelline cried. "Open it. Open it!"

"Er errrrr er," Trucker replied.

"Okay den," Long John shrugged, "suit yerselves but don't say I didn't warn yas."

He stepped aside so the others could go before him.

Trucker put his hand on the knob and turned it. The door squeakily opened to reveal complete and total darkness. A damp and musty odor encompassed them.

"Ghosties!" Daphney screamed, before flying past the group and back up the stairs.

Trucker jumped at the scream, and let the door go. Its uneven hinges caused it to swing away from them and hit the cement wall with a deafening bang. Everyone jumped and screamed—including Ponder—who had somehow managed to do it at the same speed as the rest.

Each member began to scramble up the stairs at the same time, trying to crawl over one another. Long John tripped immediately, and the others climbed over him, to make their escape. Although Daphney made it to the top first, Trucker managed to outrun her to the garage door. He shimmied under it and back outside. He watched as Daphney appeared, followed by Maybelline, Lorelei, Long John, and finally, Ponder.

"Ghosties," Daphney whispered again, the whites of her wide eyes showing in the dark.

"Yep," Maybelline agreed, "there's ghostises in there alright."

Lorelei, bent over trying to catch her breath. She bobbed her head too. Ponder looked at Long John, who shrugged. Trucker hesitantly bent over to sneak a peek back under the garage door to make sure they hadn't been followed by their unseen nemesis.

"Errr er errrr errr," Trucker instructed Long John, who walked over to the door and helped Trucker close it.

"Er errr er er errr," Trucker turned to his cohorts.

"Trucker wants ta go home," Long John reported.

Daphney took off running as fast as she could, her white cotton nightgown flapping behind her.

After the ghost encounter the small band laid low for about two weeks before they gained the courage to venture out again. Exactly as they had done on that first night, they strategically assembled themselves as well as any top secret military group, sneaking into enemy territory.

Once outside, Trucker erred, outlining the night's plans.

"We'rea gonna go en git some apples," Long John relayed. "Trucker saw a big ole tree of 'em down tha road." He pointed north on the old highway, which ran in front of Tinsley's.

"Ohhhhh goody! I love apples." Maybelline smacked her lips.

"Me too," Lorelei agreed.

"Too," Daphney giggled.

Trucker hitched up his droopy britches and started walking toward the road, the crunch of gravel under his boots called out into the still night.

As they passed the house where Ole Pete, an very old Cherokee Indian, had once lived with his sister, Ponder stopped and stared at the house.

"I...wish...we's...could...go...talk...to...Old...Pete," Ponder stalely remarked,

Long John nodded.

"I sure do like Old Pete," Long John agreed. "He lives back thur somewhere."

Long John pointed to the woods behind the small and dark clapboard house.

"Let's go find him!" Lorelei exclaimed.

"Errrr," Trucker interjected.

"Snakes," Long John agreed.

"Snakes," Daphney whispered, her eyes wide with fear.

"Uh uh. I ain't goin' if there's snakes." Maybelline shook her head.

"Lets…jest…go…en…gets…summa…dem…apples."

Ponder slowly licked his lips as he headed toward the paved highway.

When the group got to the road, Long John stuck his arm out to make everyone halt.

"We's gotta look both ways fer we cross," he ordered.

Daphney, Lorelei, and Maybelline all shook their heads in agreement, while Trucker pushed Long John's arm out of the way, and haughtily sauntered past him.

"You're gonna get hit," Maybelline gasped.

Trucker turned and erred at her before continuing to make his way across the dark and desolate road. Long John shrugged and followed, then motioned for the rest to come along.

Trucker hadn't waited on the others and was already past Jumper Creek, which ran under the road and came out the other side. He impatiently turned around to make sure he was being followed. When he realized the group had stopped to look over the road at the small creek below, he retraced his steps and angrily erred at them.

"He said ta come on," Long John sighed, then turned to join Trucker.

The group ambled along the gravel shoulder of the highway, making their way past the small one-room Living God Pentecostal of Holiness Church, and past the overgrown weeds, which were taller than most them. About thirty yards further, they stepped onto a neatly manicured lawn which was flanked by white post and rail fencing.

Trucker boldly marched to the waist high fence and climbed over. The rest of the group stalled, looking back and forth from him, to the wide open driveway a few feet away.

Lorelei was the first to split from the group and use the gravel drive instead of the fence. Trucker erred his displeasure, so Long John took the harder route. The rest however, opted for the easy access and skipped through the large opening.

A large white, and well maintained plantation style home sat about a hundred feet back at the end of the circular drive. It had green shutters, and a green roof. Daphney was quite taken with it.

"Pretty," she pointed. "Pretty, pretty."

"Yeah, it's extra big." Maybelline began walking toward it.

"Let's live here!" Lorelei interjected excitedly.

"I...don't...think...we's...can." Ponder pointed to two adjacent windows on the south end of the bottom floor.

"Someone...already...be...livin'...here. See,...there's... lights...on."

Trucker ignored them, and headed halfway into the yard toward a large apple tree, north of the driveway.

"Err er," he said over his shoulder.

"He said ta come on," Long John reported.

"No, let's go see who lives here." Lorelei began walking toward the light.

Much to Trucker's dismay, the rest of the party followed her.

"Errrrr!" he called out to them as they passed.

Long John paused, torn between his friend, and his curiosity. It was only a few seconds though, before curiosity won and he called back to Trucker.

"Let's jest look real quick like, then we's kin git us 'em apples."

Trucker huffed his displeasure, but followed the slim man toward the house.

Lorelei, marched up to the first window without a shred of fear, and peered inside.

"Ohhhh," she looked back at the others. "It's got a fireplace."

"Let my see," Daphney pushed her aside, and poked her own nose to the cool window pane. "Ohhhh," she echoed Lorelei's sentiment.

"Move over," Maybelline ordered them both, and shoved herself between the two.

"It does," she turned and whispered to the men. "And look," she pointed toward the opposite wall, "there's a man in there too."

Lorelei and Daphney followed her finger to see an elderly man sitting in an overstuffed brown leather chair. He had a newspaper folded on his lap while he held the end of a black wooden smoking pipe in his mouth.

"That's a pipe," Maybelline reported. "Somebody I once knowed had one." She sighed as if she had been transported back in time.

"Errr er err," Trucker pushed his way between the girls, and motioned for Long John and Ponder to follow. The two obliged without discussion.

"Errr, errr, err." Trucker whispered.

"I wants one too," Long John acknowledged.

"Me...too," Ponder acquiesced.

"Me," Daphney joined, although she wasn't really sure she did.

The group stood quietly gazing at the tired looking man, while he smoked his pipe, until Trucker remembered their real mission and poked Long John. He gestured for him to follow along to the apple tree.

"Come on ya'll, itsa time ta git sum apples," he relayed.

Everyone turned to leave, except Maybelline, who continued to watch the old man. A solitary tear slipped down her puffy pink cheek.

Chapter Six

From time to time, Maybelline would remember her life before she had lived at Tinsleys, but it only came in small spurts of pictures—most of which didn't make sense to her.

The pictures could be triggered by a comment, a picture, or a smell—especially food smells. One day, when the cafeteria had chicken and dumplings, she had a flash of an older woman with a pink apron on. She was stirring a large pot that sat atop a white stove.

When the cooks made brown beans, or extra buttery mashed potatoes, she would see the same thing.

Maybelline couldn't remember who the woman was, but she could remember the worn, grayish, leather house slippers that she wore on her feet. She also remembered sitting on a step ladder stool, watching the plump lady as she cooked.

But one memory in particular would send a warm feeling through her heart. It was when the woman would stop her scurrying, long enough to get eye level with the girl, then stroke her hair, and kiss her nose.

There were other memories too. But they didn't involve the plump woman, and they didn't give her a warm feeling. In fact, they often sent shivers up her spine.

They were of another, younger woman. One with reddish-brown hair, who often frowned at her. Maybelline remembered the older woman taking her from the younger one. The plump one had scowled at the red haired woman while waving her away and telling her to "Git on outta here," and "If you aren't gonna take care of her, I will."

Her most vivid memory though was when she awoke one morning and the older woman hadn't come to get her out of the small cot-like bed in which she had been sleeping.

Maybelline had whined to let the woman know she was awake. Her noise usually triggered the room's door opening, and the woman coming to scoop her up and kiss her cheek. But on that morning, she hadn't come. After a few moments of being ignored, Maybelline began to cry. The door still didn't open.

She couldn't remember if it was fear, or another thing that let her know something wasn't right. When whatever that feeling was had come over her, she panicked, squealing, and wailing. She sat atop the bed hoping that the feeling was wrong, and that the woman would come rushing in to comfort her, but her cries changed nothing.

Maybelline couldn't remember how long she had cried, but she knew she had finally fallen back asleep only to awaken to a still empty room. She could hear voices through the door, and she immediately began to wail again. This time the door flung open so hard that it slammed against the wall. It startled Maybelline so badly that she began to cry even harder.

The red-haired woman entered the room with the familiar scowl, and harshly grabbed the child, shaking her.

"Shut up," she ordered. "Just shut up, cause there ain't no one here that's gonna put up with your bellyaching."

Then she threw Maybelline onto the larger bed in the room and told her to sit there until she was told to get up. Maybelline had sniffled, trying to keep the tears, and her whimpers at bay. She needed to pee badly.

She wanted to tell the woman, but she was too afraid. She held her pee until it hurt, and her tears began to coat her cheeks again. She did not want to upset the woman, although she could now not remember why. She tried with everything not to pee herself, but the pain was torturous. Before she knew what had happened, she felt herself sitting in a warm puddle, her pajama bottoms and the bedding soaked.

She remembered that she was very scared, and she remembered not knowing what she should do. She heard the woman coming from the next room, and she instinctively hid under the bed. When the woman came in, she screamed at her.

"What the hell did you do you little brat? Where the hell are you?"

Maybelline remembered shivering and feeling very sick to her stomach, but she didn't remember what happened after that.

The old man Maybelline had seen through the window, reminded her of a similar one that had lived in the same house as the two women. She remembered that he often threw her in the air, both of them giggling, as she came back down and into his arms. She remembered that he always had a piece of Juicy Fruit gum just for her, and she remembered sitting on his lap and touching his prickly face. He would laugh when she would pull her surprised hand back after she had done it.

He too had smoked a pipe, and he would take its bowl and poke her on the nose with it, causing her to grin. She knew she loved him fiercely, but she couldn't remember who he was.

After the day that the old woman didn't come get her, Maybelline never saw any of them again. She remembered being dropped off by the red-haired woman at a hospital like place, but it wasn't anything like Tinsleys. There were other children—like her—who were there, but there were also ones that were worse.

Those children had been left sitting in floor of the hallways. They wore diapers, even though they were bigger than she was. She remembered that they smelled very bad. Most of the time, they would be left there all day. Some of them drooled, and did nothing more than stare at a dirty white ceiling. She once had tried to talk to one of them, but he never even noticed her, and the stench that surrounded him was unbearable for more than just a moment. After that, she didn't try to make friends with the ones in the hall anymore.

Maybelline couldn't recall how long she had stayed at the place, she only remembered how happy she was to leave it.

She had been at her new home for very long time and the longer she was at Tinsleys the easier her old memories faded.

It frustrated her that she couldn't remember the old man and the old woman any better. It upset her that no one had ever come to visit her or bring her a birthday or Christmas present.

Ever since Daphney had moved in, Daphney's sister, Susie, had brought Maybelline a Christmas present. She was the only one who ever had.

Susie asked her once on which day was her birthday, but Maybelline didn't know. Sometimes, she pretended it was on the same day as some of the other residents. She liked it that way, because it meant that she got to have a lot of birthdays in the year. The cooks would always let her have a cupcake if she told them it was her birthday too. It all worked out fine.

≻o≺

Maybelline realized there were more tears running down her check. She wiped them away, then sighed heavily, taking one last look at the man in the chair before turning to catch up with her friends.

Chapter Seven

After turning their pajama tops into make-shift satchels and filling them with apples, the group followed Trucker over to a large pond several yards north of the big white house. The bullfrogs stopped their incessant crocking as the interlopers arrived.

"Dey...don't...like...us...here," Ponder informed the rest.

Lorelei looked around quickly and backed up as if ready to run.

"Who don't want us here?" her eyes bugged with fear.

"Ghosties?" Daphney whispered.

Ponder shook his head. "Naw," he waved her off, "jest... da... bullfrogs."

The six formed a circle. Daphney continued to search the darkness, wary of any ghosts who might be lurking in the shadows. The rest sat down and put their apples in the middle.

"It's okay Daphney." Maybelline patted the ground next to her and motioned for her friend to sit down.

"It's just them frogs that Ponder was talking about. Let's eat our apples!" She giddily clapped her hands.

Daphney complied and the group began to grab at the pile of apples before them. For several minutes the only sounds around them—besides some chirping crickets—was the munching and crunching of the small green fruit.

When Trucker took his first bite, he twisted his mouth and shut one eye.

"Errr," he looked to Long John.

"Yeah, thur sour alright," he agreed.

Before long the bullfrogs had commenced their songs of unrequited love, as the group continued to gorge themselves on some of the best fruit they had ever had.

Food at Tinsleys didn't just leave a lot to be desired; it left everything to be desired. The only fruit the residents were served was fruit cocktail, stewed peaches, prunes or applesauce.

The fruit wasn't the worst of the bad food either. Most of the meals consisted of very bland and soft foods that the older residents could easily chew and digest.

The bad food was one of the reasons the Tinsleys loved to walk into to town. There they could get wonderful barbeque sandwiches from Pendleton's, Olive Loaf sandwiches from Ralph's, or a cheeseburger from the Eater Upper. Trucker and Long John also were able to get their favorite thing in the world at Stephen's Drug—Double Bubble Bubble Gum. Their love of it meant that they usually would go to town daily, except Sundays, when the drugstore was closed.

"I…wanna…get…me…a…frog," Ponder thought aloud.

The rest of the Tinsleys stopped munching their fruit and looked at him. Long John was the first to respond.

"Howda we do thet?"

"Yous…has…to…sneak…up…on…'em."

Maybelline cocked her head to the side and bit her lower lip. "I'm a good sneaker," she informed her friends. "I sneak cookies from the cafeteria all the time."

"Er err," Trucker replied.

"Yep," Long John nodded, "we's do too."

"Sneak frog."

Daphney got up from her sitting position and looked down at the rest of them.

Ponder slowly arose too, followed by Lorelei.

"How we gonna sneak up on them Ponder?" Maybelline asked.

"Yous…jest…gets…in…da…water…en…swims…real …slow…like…up…to…'em. Dens…yous…grabs…'em." He slowly clutched his hands together making a hollow clapping sound.

Daphney had already headed toward the water's edge, discarding her house shoes before she got there. She stuck a toe in then quickly pulled it out.

"Cold," she turned to inform the group.

"It…gets…warm…after…ya…gets…in."

75

Ponder walked toward her and bent over removing his own leather slippers. Then he slowly walked into the pond. He loudly sucked in his breath as his foot submerged. "It's... cold...alright," he agreed, but continued his trek into the darkness.

Before anyone knew what had happened, a streak went flying past, followed by a loud splash, and a high-pitched, but grunting squeal.

"Truckers done en gone in." Long John pointed at the grinning bald head sticking out from the pond's surface.

"Err er!" Trucker ordered.

"He says ta git in," Long John announced.

In only a few short seconds the still night air was broken with splashes and screeching, which promptly halted when the front porch light of the big white house illuminated.

"Shhhh!" Lorelei put her finger to her mouth and warned the group, "We're gonna get caught."

No one moved a muscle as they watched the old man open the door and walk out onto the porch. He went to the front of the columned structure, placing his hand above his eyes. He peered into the darkness. Then he moved to the farthest edge of the porch and did the same thing. Finally, he came to the side closest to the interlopers.

He scanned the field toward the road, and then scanned the horizon of the pond. Every last Tinsley held their breath, hoping not to be seen. After a few short moments of standing there, the old man turned and walked away, reentering his home, and turning off the light.

"We's better git goin'," Long John told the others. "He may be wantin' ta call tha po-leeze."

"Po... leeze," Daphney echoed.

"Errr," Trucker cursed, as he waved for the rest of them to follow him out of the pond.

"We're all wet," Maybelline declared when they had all exited.

"Um hm,...wet," Ponder agreed.

"We gonna be dry by the time we get back," Lorelei surmised. "Let's get the apples and take 'em with us!"

Everyone bent over to retrieve their fruit, and then soggily, followed Trucker back to the edge of the road, and toward their home.

As they again passed the house where old Pete had once lived, it was Trucker this time who commented.

"Er errr err." He stopped to stare at the house.

"Why ya miss 'em?" Long John asked.

Trucker kicked the dead grass and rocks on the shoulder of the road, but he didn't answer.

Trucker knew he was the reason old Pete had left, but out of guilt, he never told anyone.

Several years previously, on a hot summer afternoon, he had gone to see Old Pete. Trucker had visited the old Indian many times and really enjoyed their chats, although Trucker had been the only one chatting.

Most of the time, Old Pete would just nod as Trucker droned on and on, about whatever it was that Trucker droned about. The fact that Old Pete even gave him the time of day, and never once asked him to repeat himself, made Trucker feel a kinship with the man. He believed that Old Pete was the only other soul on the planet—besides Long John—who truly understood him.

The day of that final visit, Trucker greeted the withered old man. Old Pete was sitting in his creaking rocking chair, looking off into the distance. His hands were busy carving a stone that he was holding.

Although Pete didn't acknowledge him, Trucker plopped down on the top step and began a long winded tirade. Trucker had talked to Pete no less than thirty minutes when, in a moment of vulnerability, he confessed to Pete that he was very fond of him, and so happy that they had become friends. Pete didn't respond.

Starting to feel embarrassed, Trucker, turned to look at him. Pete was still staring off in the distance and remained silent.

Trucker awkwardly shifted his weight, starting to feel as if Pete didn't want to be his friend. Several more seconds passed without an acknowledgment.

It had not been easy for Trucker to admit his feelings towards Old Pete. He had never even been brave enough to tell Long John how he felt about him, because of something that happened the first—and only—time, he had done so with another.

Trucker was only a teenager when he had met Bertha, a fellow resident of the mental facility in Vinita. Bertha was a few years Trucker's senior. From the moment Trucker had first laid eyes on her, he was smitten. Smitten was probably too mild a word. He was actually head over heels in love.

Bertha had been brought into the home in a wheelchair. She was chubby like Trucker, with chocolate brown hair. She also had the biggest, richest, brown eyes he had ever seen.

Trucker watched her as she was checked into the facility. Then he followed the orderlies as they wheeled Bertha down the hall to her new room. Trucker loitered several feet away from the door as they unpacked her clothing and settled her.

When the orderlies left, Trucker tiptoed to Bertha's door and peeked his head inside. Bertha spotted him immediately. Trucker shyly smiled. Bertha didn't respond except to look around, as if she was looking for help.

Trucker walked inside, and erred a greeting. Bertha, somewhat alarmed, and hoping the homely boy would go away, remained silent.

Trucker pulled up a chair and immediately began telling Bertha all about the home. After several minutes of his incessant, and incomprehensible, erring, Bertha tried to save herself.

"Help?" she said as an orderly passed her room.

The man, too self-absorbed to realize he was being summoned, continued on his way, while Trucker continued his oration.

When the same orderly passed by again, Bertha yelled louder.

"HEY! Help me!"

The man jumped then entered her room.

"What?"

Bertha pointed to the still rambling Trucker.

The orderly knowingly nodded.

"Come on Harold," he ordered, grabbing Trucker by the arm and lifting him from the chair, "You need to let this young lady settle in before you start your nonsense."

Trucker got up but continued erring important information as the orderly drug him out the door.

After that first encounter, Bertha scarcely found herself alone. No matter where she went— from the time she got out of bed in the morning, to the time she went to sleep—Trucker was by her side following her everywhere.

Bertha tried to remain patient, hoping that if she continued to ignore Trucker's feeble attempts at romance, he would tire of her and move along. That wasn't to be.

It had taken Trucker months to work up the courage to tell Bertha how he felt about her—that she was his one true love. Unfortunately for Trucker, that day had coincided with Bertha finally hitting her Trucker limit.

Bertha, as was her custom, had gone outside to sit in the sun. Trucker plopped himself down on a wooden park bench next to her. For once in his life, his nerves got the best of him and he sat in silence for several minutes before he cleared his throat and began to speak.

"Er…" he tried to confess, but he began stumbling over everything he was trying to say. Bertha had never once understood a single thing Trucker had ever said to her, so as was her custom, she completely ignored him.

Trucker, not realizing his words were in vain, became more embarrassed as he tried to explain his feelings. He flushed bright red, and his hands began to sweat profusely, but he finally got the words out that he had longed to say to her since the day they had first met.

As soon as he did, he waited in intense anticipation for Bertha to tell him that she returned his feelings, and that he, too, was the love of her life.

Instead, Bertha remained silent, watching the goings on around her and paying absolutely no mind to the dwarfish man beside her.

Trucker was crushed that Bertha obviously didn't share his feelings. He became livid when he noticed that his paramour, was instead, dreamily smiling at Benny Strong.

Benny was a slightly older, and much taller resident who also happened to be Trucker's greatest foe.

Trucker jumped out of his seat and loudly "Erred" at his nemesis. Then he stood between Bertha and Benny so she could no longer see her crush. He turned back to Bertha and commenced to erring his disdain at her for ignoring his proclamation of pure unadulterated love.

That's when Bertha let him have it.

"Harold, I have had enough of you!" She slapped at him,

"I'm sick and tired of you following me around everywhere I go! I'm sick and tired of you forever talking your gibberish to me! You need to find someone else to pester and LEAVE ME ALONE!"

Trucker had no idea she felt that way about him. He had assumed that since she hadn't told him to go away sooner, that she actually liked him too. His face turned an even deeper shade of crimson. His hands not only continued to sweat, but also began to shake. For once in his life, he couldn't bring himself to say anything. Instead, he dropped his head in shame.

Trucker wanted more than anything to run as far away from Bertha and Benny—who he could now hear snickering—but, his legs wouldn't work. He stood there in his embarrassment, praying that Bertha would at least put him out of his misery and leave herself.

He sighed in relief when just a few seconds later, she did. He lifted his head and watched her turn her wheelchair around and roll toward Benny.

A tear slipped from Trucker's eyes when he heard

her call out to Benny. "You want to get a soda?"

≻o≺

The day that Trucker had exposed his feelings to Old Pete and got no response in return, he felt his face get hot. The entire episode with Bertha flooded his mind and he felt ridiculous all over again. He shoved Old Pete who, in reflex, took the knife he was holding, and almost stabbed Trucker with it.

It was then that Trucker saw complete surprise and terror in Old Pete's eyes. Old Pete wasn't ignoring him. He hadn't heard him. He must have been day dreaming—much like Trucker would sometimes do when he remembered his old life back in Vinita.

Trucker tried to apologize. "Er errrr," he backed down the steps. Old Pete, still in a state of shock," got up from his rocking chair, and ambled into his house. Trucker meekly returned to the home.

The next day, Trucker came back to apologize again, but Old Pete wasn't there. Pete's sister told him, and two other Tinsleys that had followed Trucker, that Old Pete had moved.

Trucker lowered his head in shame, knowing it was all his fault that his friend left.

>o<

The group was still wet by the time they had made the ten minute walk back to Tinsley's. They sloshed back through the emergency exit and each went to their rooms to get in dry pajamas.

"Bring tha wet uns back here," Long John ordered them.

When each met back at the door with their soaked clothing, Long John directed them back out the door.

"Hang 'em here ta dry," he pointed to the chain link fence which surrounded most of the property.

The group did as they were told, each laying the clothing across the long metal bar at the top. Then they returned to their rooms and went to bed.

The following morning they were awoken to the sound of several aides and orderlies outside their rooms.

"Did you guys see this?" Lorelei heard a large and scruffy orderly named Darrel ask.

"Where'd you get that stuff?" she heard a nurse named Linda reply.

"It was all layin' across the fence," Darrell answered.

"Whose is it?" an aide questioned.

"No idea," Darrell responded.

"Well get it to the laundry and don't let the Charge Nurse know. She'll have our asses," Linda replied.

Lorelei smiled a knowing smile, and turned back over to sleep.

Chapter Eight

Most of the time the group of Tinsleys passed their days running up and down the halls, playing with stuffed animals and puzzles in the play room, or watching *Sesame Street*. All, that is, except for Trucker. Trucker hated stuffed animals, and he hated with a passion, *Sesame Street*.

When the gang was gathered each afternoon at three-thirty to watch it, Trucker was left alone and he was bored. He would go to the playroom and try to get Long John to join him outside, or to go into town.

"Errr."

He would stand at the door and motion for Long John but his skinny friend was so engrossed with Burt and Ernie or Cookie Monster, that he wouldn't even hear him.

"ERRRRRRR!" Trucker would yell, but Long John remained oblivious.

Finally in his frustration, Trucker would march over to Long John and stand in front of him, blocking his view of the television. Long John would swat at him, trying to get him to move. Trucker would never oblige. Instead, he would bend down to eye level and errr loudly again.

"Imma watchin' *Sesame Street*." Long John would furrow his brow in frustration. Trucker would ignore him, and errr while poking Long John on the chest.

"Stop it," Long John would try to dodge Trucker's roly-poly belly so he could see around him.

"Er errr Errrrr Errr!" Trucker would purse his lips to show his disdain.

"I knows ya hate *Sesame Street*," Long John stated, as he continued to try to see around the nuisance, "but iffin ya'd jest try watchin' it, ya'd like it."

"ER!" Trucker yelled, causing the rest of the watching residents to turn and glare at him.

"I ain't goin' ta town wid ya tils Imma done watchin' *Sesame Street*," Long John would proclaim. Then he would report whatever his good reason for the day was.

"Thur gonna sing *Rubber Ducky* and I ain't going tils itsa over!" Then he would push Trucker aside and sit back down, gluing his eyes to the screen.

Finally defeated, Trucker would stomp his foot and yell at the top of his lungs. He would leave the small room, erring a string of Trucker style profanities as he went.

Trucker hated *Sesame Street* with good reason. It was his only competition. From the time he had moved into Tinsley's, and Long John had arrived, Trucker had been the ring leader of all able bodied Tinsleys. He spent a great amount of time scheming, and conniving ways to wreak havoc upon his enemies—also known as the staff.

Trucker was more than proficient at getting his followers to do most of his dirty work. Than is until *Sesame Street* had come on the air almost seven years earlier, Trucker had been pushed aside five days a week in favor of the annoying puppets. One day, his disdain came to a head.

For Christmas the previous year, Daphney had been given a stuffed Big Bird. Trucker wanted more than anything to tear its rotten head off. A couple of weeks after she got it, he made it the target of his frustration.

Trucker was ready to have his afternoon meeting of the minds, and had gone in search of his posse. As usual, he found them glued to the television set, singing along with the *ABC Song*.

"Errr er," he yelled from the doorway.

Long John turned to look at him. "Not yet, Trucker. We's watching *Sesame Street*."

"ERRRRR!" Trucker demanded.

"Uh uh." Long John shook his head without turning to look at Trucker.

Trucker was livid. He marched over to Daphney and Lorelei's room and grabbed the stuffed bird. Then he marched back to the play room and planted himself right in front of the TV. He took Big Bird and swung him around his head and then abruptly stopped, and commenced to trying to pull its head off.

Daphney screamed and jumped to her feet, lunging at Trucker. Lorelei, ever Daphney's protector, did the same. Before anyone knew what was happening, there was a whirling, twirling ball of Tinsleys and yellow bird, careening across the room.

Most of the other Tinsleys paid no mind to the disturbance and mesmerized, continued watching the program. However, the screams from both Daphney and Lorelei, alerted the staff. Three of them came plowing through the door at the same time.

"What the heck is going on in here?!" Margie Poleman, a heavyset, grandmotherly type black woman, and the charge nurse, screamed. She raced around the rows of chairs trying to get to the middle of the commotion.

Trucker, playing keep away from the two girls, held the bird as high above his short head as he could. Both continued their screaming.

"Er errr Errrrrrr Errrrr!" he yelled at everyone.

"He hates *Sesame Street*," Long John interpreted, without taking his eyes off the television.

"Trucker, you give Daphney her Big Bird right this minute!" Margie yelled at the raging Tinsley.

Trucker ignored her, and continued his taunting.

"Get him," Margie told Randy Adams, a very tall, and pasty, cotton headed, aide.

Randy made his own way around the chairs, and all the residents congregated in front of the television. Then he tried herding the three whirling dervishes toward the corner of the room, where he could trap them.

Trucker screamed again about hating *Sesame Street* and every time Daphney or Lorelei tried to grab the toy from him, he jumped with the bird high over his head

Randy the aide, pointed to his left side and addressed the other staff.

"You guys trap them there; I'll get them into the corner and get the bird."

When Trucker heard this, he stopped jumping long enough to assess the situation. He was already almost in the corner, and saw that he wasn't likely going to be able to escape the grasp of Randy.

In a split second, he threw the bird at the aide. Randy instinctively threw up his hands to catch it, and Trucker slipped beneath his arms, and out the door through the unmanned side of the corner. As soon as he passed through the door, he turned around, red faced and hollered again.

"Er errr Errrrr Errrr er errr err!"

"He hates *Sesame Street* and he hates you," Long John told Randy.

Randy shook his head and turned to give Daphney back her bird, which she greedily grabbed and hugged to her chest.

"That one is gonna be the death of me," Randy told Margie.

"Oh, you ain't the only one who's gonna suffer demise at the hands of that little rabble-rouser." Margie put her hands on her hips and sighed. "We all goin' down in flames together."

Daphney continued protecting Big Bird, keeping him close, while she grabbed Lorelei's hand and led her back to their chairs. They both plopped down and began counting in unison with Count von Count and the rest of the room

"One, ah ha ha; two, ah ha ha; three, ah ha ha."

Trucker could be still heard all the way down the hall, still proclaiming his animosity for *Sesame Street*.

>o<

On this day, Trucker had come up with an ingenious idea and he was not willing to wait any longer to initiate his plan. He was about to tip Long John out of his chair, but as luck would have it, *Sesame Street* ended.

Trucker frowned at the room's viewers, as they got up, smiling and singing to themselves.

"Sunny Days, everything's A-Okay."

Trucker erred as they passed him. Then he cleared his throat to address his minions.

"Errr errr."

"Trucker said 'come hurr,'" Long John told the group.

While they gathered in the corner of the room, Trucker whispered to Long John, who in turn whispered to the rest, that Trucker had a very secret plan. He also told them that he was not allowed to share it with anyone until he and Trucker had gone into town to get supplies.

The group began to get excited, but they all knew better than to test Trucker's patience. They begrudgingly nodded their heads and then dispersed.

Chapter Nine

Trucker and Long John returned to their room and got the money they each had stashed in their nightstands. As they stuffed little wads of bills into their pockets, Long John felt his stomach rumble. He looked at the clock on the nightstand.

"Supper's in jest en hour," he told Trucker. "We's not gonna be back en time. Maybe we's should go tumarra."

Trucker grunted, and shook his head no. He wasn't going to let anything stand in the way of his mission.

"Errr errr er errrr," he growled.

"I knows tha food here is crappy," Long John agreed. "But Imma hungry."

"Errr err errrrrrrrrrrrr." "

Long John perked up.

"Yeah, we's kin go git cheeseburgers," he agreed. "We'll go ta tha Eater Upper on tha way home."

The two determinedly walked past the nurses' station, and out the front door. By the time they got to the old highway, Trucker was skipping and talking a mile a minute. Long John was bent over trying to hear every word, and occasionally nodding in agreement.

It took the men about ten minutes to pass the curve into town and make it to the corner of State and Main Street. Just across the street sat the first of the town's buildings. The structure was a tiny little service station with only one garage.

Long John stuck out his arm to keep Trucker from sprinting across the road, and directly into the path of the only oncoming car. It was driven by Mrs. Belle.

Long John knew, from countless previous encounters with the silver-haired woman, that she was the most dangerous driver in the whole town. In fact, he always strove to stay at least twenty feet from the road if he saw her coming.

Sure enough, within seconds of him spotting her, the purplish-maroon Ford Fairlane began crossing the faded yellow line. It was headed straight for them. Long John pulled

Trucker back just as the car swooped around them, taking the corner like a bat out of hell.

Severely irritated, Trucker shook his fist and yelled after the little woman.

"Errr err errrr! Err's errrr!"

"Its was too close," Long John agreed. "But I don't think she's crazy. I keeps tellin' ya thet she can't see over thet thur wheel."

Trucker erred his displeasure with Long John's failure to agree with him, but it wasn't long before the two composed themselves. Long John grabbed Trucker's arm and led him across the street, past the first station, then the railroad tracks, and on to Harvey's, a larger service station.

Trucker stopped beneath a sign which displayed a big green dinosaur. He looked up at it admiringly.

"Er errr err er errrr," he pointed up to it.

"Me too," Long John agreed. "We cud own tha world iffin we had us a dinosaur."

The two friends revered the sign a few more moments before they made the turn up the main street in the town, which was actually called Broadway. It was only a few moments before they reached their destination—Oklahoma Tire and Supply, also known as OTASCO. A small bell sounded as they swung open the glass door.

"What's up there fellas?"

Earl Warren, the store's owner, came from behind the cash register, which was located near the rear of the shop. He sauntered up the aisle to greet them.

"Er errr errr," Trucker stated.

"We need rope," Long John said.

"Rope huh?"

Earl looked the two misfits up and down before deciding the rope was harmless enough, and that he could sell it to them.

"Watcha need rope for?" he asked, as he turned to lead them toward the back of the store.

Long John looked at Trucker to see if they should divulge their plans. Trucker shook his head no.

"Um," Long John tried to stall, "we's gonna build us a clothesline."

He grinned at Trucker, proud that he had managed to lie so quickly.

"A clothesline huh?"

"Er er," Trucker answered.

"Um hm," Long John echoed.

"Here it is boys." Earl pointed to a gray metal shelf on their left. It held several ropes coiled inside of cellophane wrapping.

"For a clothesline you ain't gonna need the heavy duty stuff. This here nylon is gonna work just fine."

Earl grabbed a white coil off the shelf, and tossed it to Long John.

"ER!"

Trucker grabbed Earl's arm, which made him jump back.

Earl had always been leery of Trucker, because he too, had been a victim of Trucker's pickup truck fetish. In fact, Earl held the town record for the longest standoff with Trucker.

Earl had been negotiating with Trucker for him to leave his truck for over forty minutes. Trucker spent the majority of that time throwing a monumental fit. In fact, Trucker had worked himself into a complete tizzy. He was jumping up and down so hard in the truck bed that Earl thought his shocks would burst. That's when he went back inside his store and called Lester, the town's only police officer.

Lester, an extremely short and obese man, waddled up to the back of the bed.

"Now Trucker, dadgummit, what in tarnation are you doing in Earl's truck? You know ya ain't supposed to get in people's trucks!"

Trucker erred like a madman and glared at Lester.

"You don't scare me none Trucker. Now you get outta the bed and you get outta there now or I'm calling Mr. Tinsley."

Trucker's shoulders sank. He remained in his standoff a few more moments until Lester told Earl to go inside and call Mr. Tinsley. Only then did Trucker surrender and reluctantly climb over the truck's tailgate.

As soon as he hit the ground he turned to Earl.

"Er're errrr er errrr."

Long John interpreted. "Ya's gonna be sorry."

Earl thought for sure he would be.

Trucker had not forgotten Earl's poor treatment of him and made it a point to spit on the store window whenever he walked by.

"Errrr," Trucker now calmly replied.

"Bigger," Long John repeated.

Earl looked the two Tinsleys over, but not wanting a repeat of Trucker's past behavior, shrugged and put the rope back on the shelf.

"Bigger it is. Come on over to this side." He motioned for the two to follow him.

When they reached the other side, Earl picked up a yellow rope, which was clearly thicker than the previous one. When he handed it to Long John, its weight almost caused the skinny man to drop it. Long John looked at Trucker who nodded his approval.

"We'll take this un," Long John told Earl.

"Okie Dokie. Anything else I can get you boys?"

Long John looked at Trucker, who in return leaned into him and whispered. Long John's surprised look scared Earl a little.

"We's needs glue too," he imparted.

Earl scratched his head, wondering how far he should let the shopping expedition go.

"Glue huh? What kinda glue?"

Long John, still unsure himself of Trucker's unfolding plan, looked back to his friend for guidance. Trucker pursed his lips and stared at the ceiling in deep thought.

"Err err errrr errrrr errr," he told them.

"Tha really sticky kind," Long John relayed.

"Um, the really sticky kind huh?" Earl tried to stifle a laugh. "Okay, let's go over here, and I'll show ya what I got."

Earl led the adventurous duo to the last aisle located in a dark corner.

"I have the regular Elmer's." He pointed to a white, blue and orange bottle. "Here I got this newfangled stuff called Liquid Nails. It's supposed to be pretty darn good at holding stuff together—but it's a lot more expensive," he added.

"Errr err!" Trucker yelled, startling both Long John and Earl.

"Thet one," Long John pointed to the Liquid Nails.

Earl was beginning to get really worried about the two Tinsleys having access to something that may cause a mess bigger than any of them could clean up. He felt as though he was obligated to search for more information.

"Ya say you're gonna put up a clothes line?" He cocked his head to the side. "Why do ya need glue?"

Again, Long John looked to his side kick, who loudly growled. He turned back to Earl and shrugged.

Earl weighed his options only a moment before Trucker growled again, and lunged toward the store owner.

Earl jumped back and put up his hands.

"Okay, okay, just askin'." He backed away from the aggressive Tinsley.

Earl motioned for the two to go ahead of him to the register, refusing to be in the lead, so that Trucker could not get the jump on him. He rang up the rope and glue.

"That'll be four-fifty," he told Long John who was already fishing through his Wrangler blue jeans pocket to get the money.

Long John pulled out a hefty handful of wadded up dollar bills and then went back in for the change he was carrying. He unloaded all of it onto the counter in front of Earl.

Earl picked through the money until he had the right amount and put it into the register drawer.

"You boys keep outta trouble now," he half-heartedly told them—knowing full well they wouldn't.

Trucker turned back and growled again.

Chapter Ten

As Trucker and Long John left the OTASCO store, Trucker pointed up and across the street to Doodle's Five and Dime.

Caught up in their mission, neither bothered to look for oncoming traffic before stepping into the street.

A blaring beep emanated from a lime green Ford Pinto, driven by sixth grade teacher Mrs. Middleton. Long John jumped at the unexpected and intrusive sound, but Trucker paid absolutely no attention, and continued on his way across the street.

Another small bell, attached to the store's door, alerted Mrs. Doodle that she had a customer. When she saw Long John, she kindly greeted him. Then she saw Trucker and backed away.

"I don't want any trouble from you Trucker, do you understand me?" she warned.

Trucker had been known to throw one of his numerous fits, if he wanted something that Mrs. Doodle didn't carry. The last time he had, it was because she didn't have any Slinkys.

Trucker had seen the contraption while watching television. He was mesmerized when it walked down stairs by itself. In his mind, it had to be alive, and although it wasn't as cute as the many stray dogs he had tried to keep, he was sure he could keep a slinky pet hidden from the same nurses who had removed his dogs.

Trucker was so excited that night that he didn't sleep a wink. He even skipped having breakfast so he could go to town and be there as soon as Doodle's opened. But when he and Long John had gotten to the little store, Mrs. Doodle told them that she had none. Trucker was inconsolable, and he threw one of the most colossal fits she had ever seen.

First, he let out a blood curdling wail, which scared the wits out of Mrs. Doodle. Then believing she must be lying to him, he began rummaging through display after display, searching for his beloved new pet. By the time he had made it to the back of the store, hundreds of rubber balls, pencils, plastic necklaces, and other sundries, were strewn all over the floor.

Mrs. Doodle had followed behind the crazed Tinsley, trying to convince him that she would order one for him, but he would not be soothed. When he finally realized there was no slinky to be had, he traded his sorrow for unabashed anger. He cursed, and threw several plastic army men at the elderly lady.

Trucker's explosion had upset Mrs. Doodle so badly that she ended up closing the store for the rest of the day so she could go home and collect her nerves.

It wasn't until the following day, when she had finally managed to calm herself, that she called the police department and told Lester what had taken place. Lester went to go see Mr. Tinsley.

"You better keep a closer eye on your Tinsleys before they really get out of hand and hurt someone real bad," he scolded.

Mr. Tinsley, ever demure, and oddly shy, shook his head as if in great remorse.

"They mean well," he explained. "I know a few of them can get a little out of hand, but they don't really mean any harm. They just want to be normal like the rest of us. I can't begrudge them that. Can you?" He turned the tables on Lester.

Lester, also a softy, acquiesced.

"I guess you're right," he sighed, "but I'm walkin' a fine line here Mr. Tinsley. I gotta keep the peace, and right now the only places where there's no peace is places with Trucker around."

Mr. Tinsley agreed to talk to Trucker. Lester reported his conversation to Mrs. Doodle, and the following day, Mr. Tinsley drove to her store and bought a hundred dollars' worth of assorted toys. Considering the hundred dollars was more than she usually sold in an entire week, Mrs. Doodle let bygones be bygones.

Mr. Tinsley took the toys to his nursing home and handed them out. Then he took Trucker aside.

"I had to go all the way to Maiden to get this," he told the wide-eyed Tinsley. "But I'm not going to give it to you unless you promise me that you are going to be better behaved when you go into town."

Trucker blinked then licked his lips, considering the proposal before him.

"Erer," he agreed.

"Trucker, I'm very serious about this," Mr. Tinsley continued. "If I get another call about the way you act, I won't do anything like this for you again. Do you understand?"

Trucker held his hands out in great anticipation and nodded his head.

Mr. Tinsley handed him a brand new Slinky and Trucker howled like a coyote, twirling around and erring his pleasure.

"Errrrr." He grinned his baby toothed grin, thanking the home's owner.

"You're welcome," the sweet man replied. "Now you run along and remember to behave yourself."

Mrs. Doodle eyed Trucker and took a deep breath, readying herself for whatever mayhem was to come. When it seemed as though he were going to behave himself, she addressed Long John, for whom she had no hard feelings.

"We're getting ready to close soon, so with what can I help you?"

Long John, clueless as to their reason for being there, turned to his friend.

"Errrr Errrrr."

Long John raised an eyebrow at the declaration, but then turned to Mrs. Doodle.

"Silly String."

Mrs. Doodle sighed with deep relief. "It's right here."

She pointed to a large display case which separated each side of the store.

"Would you like blue, pink, or green?" she asked Long John, who immediately turned to Trucker.

Trucker looked to the ceiling in thought, before deciding. "Errrr."

"Green," Long John pointed to the green can, while Mrs. Doodle retrieved it.

"Will that be all?" she continued to address Long John, coolly ignoring her adversary.

Long John again looked to Trucker, who nodded it was, and Mrs. Doodle rang up the sale with no further incidents. She almost told them to come again, but she thought better of it, and let them walk out the door with no further comment.

As soon as the two Tinsleys were out the door, Trucker informed Long John of their next stop.

"Yeah, gum," Long John agreed.

Both made their way down the street so they could get to their favorite gum supply store, Stephens Drugstore. They approached just as the store's owner was locking up for the evening.

Trucker grunted at Mary Ann Stephens, and put his hands on his hips, clearly upset.

Mary Ann, who was also the store's pharmacist, turned to look at the two men behind her.

"We're closed," she matter-of-factly stated.

"Er er," Trucker shook his head.

"Uh uh," Long John shook his head too.

"Yes we are Trucker. We are closed. Tell him Long John."

But before he could, Trucker raised his voice and menacingly erred.

"We's wants sum gum," Long John stated.

"Well I'm sorry but we're closed." She stood her ground. "You are going to have to get your gum tomorrow."

"Er er," Trucker's voice was even louder.

"Uh uh," Long John hesitantly reported.

"Uh huh," the woman insisted. "It's five after five. The lights are off, the registers are cleared out, and I'm not opening this store back up; so both of you can just get on back to Tinsley's and you can get your gum tomorrow."

Trucker eyed her for a long moment. Mary Ann knew the look well, as she had already had several years of experience with Trucker and his foolery—the worst being his attempted assault on her youngest son, Sam.

"Don't you look at me like that Trucker Tinsley," she scolded him as if she were talking to her own child. "And don't you think for one minute that you are going to start causing trouble, because I've about had it with you and your nastiness. When we came to deliver prescriptions and you tried to fight Sam, you are damn lucky I didn't thump you then."

The two remained squared off, glaring at one another, unflinchingly.

Long John, who was sure that Mary Ann might in fact thump Trucker, tried to pull his best friend away. Trucker resisted, keeping his eyes glued to the woman in front of him. Mary Ann was becoming more perturbed.

"You want to test me Trucker? Cause I don't think you do," she hissed.

She put her left hand on her hip, then pointed at him with her right.

"I don't think you want to see what it is when I mean business. I'll be all over you like a duck on a June bug," she warned the little menace.

There was no longer any doubt in Long John's mind that, indeed, Mary Ann Stephens did mean business. In fact, at that moment, she lunged and Trucker jumped back with a little shriek. Long John pulled again, and this time, Trucker went willingly, almost stumbling over his lanky friend.

"That's what I thought," Mary Ann smugly replied.

"Er errr errr err," Trucker angrily retorted.

"He don't like ya," Long John told her.

"Good, cause I don't like him either," the store owner said, as she slung the purse behind her shoulder and walked to her car. As soon as she opened the door, she turned around address the duo again.

"We just got some fresh Double Bubble today, so I'll see you boys tomorrow."

She waved, got into her car, and drove away.

"Well I guess we's jest as well go on en git us a Morty Burger." Long John looked down at Trucker.

Trucker agreed, and they headed toward the Eater Upper to get the burger that was named after Morty, the butcher at Ralph's.

Morty loved his burgers fully loaded, with added bacon, cheese, and grilled onions. It was the most expensive burger in the place at a dollar, but it was worth every penny.

Trucker and Long John continued the block and a half walk to the Eater Upper. When they came to the end of the first block, Trucker headed for the car wash that was on the corner. He walked into the first of two stalls and lifted the long wand like spray nozzle. He pointed it at Long John as if it were a rifle.

"Errr!" he yelled.

"Awwww," Long John grabbed his chest, "ya gots me."

He staggered around through the wet puddles that remained on concrete floor, almost soaking his brown and scuffed leather shoes.

"Errr!" Trucker yelled with his second make believe shot.

"Awwww, nows ya's gone en done it," Long John stumbled backwards. "Imma goner fer sure."

Trucker snickered, put the wand back in its holder, and slapped Long John on the back, before leading him on toward their dinner.

As they crossed the side street, Long John spied something in the window of the car parts store on the opposite corner. It was a glowing red, white and blue sign that read "We sell Genuine Chevy Parts."

Long John walked to the window and pressed his nose against it. He stared at the sign and let out a sigh. The place brought back memories of being a child in his dad's dusty garage, filled with cars in different states of disrepair.

Long John's dad had been a mechanic and John (as he was called back before he had shot up into his current spindly frame), had been allowed to stay at the shop when his mother, who did the books, was there.

John remembered the sounds of grinding and clanging, and the smell of grease and oil. He thought back to the vending machine that sat in the front of the office, and he smiled when he recalled his mother supplying him with a nickel so he could get a roll of wintergreen candies. John would eat the whole roll in one sitting. Next to Double Bubble, it was still his favorite treat.

He also remembered the neon sign that stayed on all day and all night. A sign exactly like the one he was looking at.

Long John had always known he was different. His parents had started him in school just like the rest of the kids his age, but they didn't let him continue after his first year— "too slow," he remembered his teacher telling his mother.

"He might be better in a home," he heard her say.

"Wadda she mean?" John questioned his mother as they left the school. "I gots a home Momma."

"Yes you do," his mother replied. "And don't you ever forget it. It's okay if they can't teach ya here, I'll teach ya," she told him.

And she tried to. She taught him his letters, but he had trouble putting them all together to make words. It just didn't make sense to him. His mother would also read to him stories of kings, and ships and even wars, but he couldn't keep them in his memory long. Still, though, he liked to hear them.

Long John smiled to himself again. Pryor Creek, Oklahoma had been where he had grown up. He hadn't been there in years—not since his momma died when he was around thirty. That was years after his daddy had already passed.

When she departed, he was completely alone, and didn't really know how to take care of himself. Mrs. Chance, their neighbor, had stayed with him the first few days, doting on him, fixing his meals and helping keep the place clean.

However, she had sat him down after that first week, and explained to him that it was only temporary because she was too old to continue. She told him that some people were coming to help him out and take him to a place where he could live with others that were like him. That's how he ended up in Vinita, about thirty miles north of his hometown. That's when he also met Trucker his very first day there.

Long John didn't like the "home" in Vinita. There were a lot of very strange people. Some sat in the corners and rocked themselves. Some stayed in their rooms and yelled. It wasn't like any home he had ever seen. It was more like the hospital he saw when his daddy was sick, but it was louder, scarier and it smelled worse.

Trucker had been outside sitting on a bench. An orderly was showing Long John around after they had given him a room and helped him put his clothes into an old wooden chest of drawers.

As he walked by the bench, Trucker eyed him up and down, making Long John a little uncomfortable.

"Er er errrrr er," Trucker had mumbled under his breath.

Long John responded.

"I ain't lookin' at ya," he lied. "I wasa jest lookin' at tha bench," he told the strange little pock marked, and burr-headed, man.

Trucker jumped up so fast that Long John took a swaying step backward. The orderly grabbed him to keep him from falling.

"Harold!" the bushy faced orderly yelled at Trucker, "You leave this man alone. This is his first day and I'm not gonna let you start messing with him."

But Trucker wasn't messing. Trucker was elated.

"You understood what I said?" Long John heard him ask.

Long John nodded that he did. Trucker lunged at Long John and wrapped him in a bear hug, although Trucker didn't even reach Long John's chest.

The orderly tried to pull Trucker off of the new resident, but Trucker only hugged Long John tighter. Long John looked at the orderly.

"Itsa okay," he informed. "He's jest glad Imma here." He smiled.

The orderly took a step back and cocked his head to the side trying to discern if what Long John said was actually true. Trucker turned around with the biggest smile he had ever seen on him. Then he watched as Trucker jumped up and down in his excitement.

"Er errr errr er errrrr!" he told the orderly.

"He says I knows what he's sayin'," Long John enlightened the man.

"You do?" He furrowed his brow.

"Yep," Long John answered, "Duddn't you?"

"Heck no." The man shook his head. "Nobody around here has a clue."

Trucker continued to smile, and then he slapped his hand on his knee and giggled.

"You really understood him?" the orderly asked Long John again.

"Uh huh," Long John nodded, finding it odd that the orderly found it odd.

"Well I'll be. In that case, I'll let Harold show you the rest of the place." The orderly shrugged and walked away.

$\succ\!\circ\!\prec$

Trucker was tugging on Long John's arm.

"Errr er. Er errrrrr."

"Okay," Long John took a step back from the window. "Imma hungry too."

The best friends turned away from the window and walked around to the front of the store. They headed to the Eater Upper to fill their bellies before they would have to return for the evening to their shared home.

Chapter Eleven

The rest of the trip to the Eater Upper was uneventful except for the short detour they had to take when they got to the funeral home. Trucker hated the funeral home. He hated the funeral home even more than he hated Sesame Street.

"Er errrr er err errerrerrerrr," he told Long John anytime they would go near it.

Long John would query each time why it gave him the heebie jeebies, and each time, Trucker would supply him with a sinister answer. On this occasion, it was that dead people would run out and eat their eyeballs.

So Long John and Trucker did what they always did, and they left the sidewalk and walked around the back of the cars parked at the curb.

When they got to the Eater Upper, the gravel parking lot was already full. Some cars were even parked out near the street in front of Harvey's Gas Station.

The smell of frying burgers, french fries, tator tots, and onion rings, permeated the air outside. Trucker rubbed his belly, and grinned his partially toothless smile. As they walked through the parked cars, they met up with John Davis, as he too was entering the greasy spoon.

"Hey there Trucker. Hey there Long John. You boys gettin' some supper too?" He took off his gray felt cowboy hat and tipped it to them.

"Err," Trucker shook his head.

"Yep," Long John translated.

"Then why don't you fellas join me? I'll buy," he offered. "Afterwards, I'll give you boys a ride back to Tinsley's."

"Erer!" Trucker accepted.

"Kay," Long John agreed.

John Davis, was in his sixties. He was a strapping man at six feet, four inches. He was liked and well respected by everyone in town. He was a rancher that lived with his wife, southwest of town, and he served on the Oklahoma Cattle Ranchers Association Board of Directors. He also served on the board of the Oklahoma State Bank and was a deacon in the First Baptist Church.

Neither Trucker, nor Long John, knew any of that; they just knew that they both liked him, albeit for different reasons.

Trucker liked John because he would give him rides in his pickup, and Long John liked him because he always spoke to him like he was just a regular person.

The three men grabbed a circular booth in the front corner of the café and slipped around to their respective places.

"Hi ya Hons."

The trio had no sooner sat down than Patty Piedmont greeted them, ready to take their order.

Patty owned the café along with her sister LaRue. LaRue was the fry cook, and Patty took orders and rang checks. The two practically lived at the small place, because they served breakfast, lunch, and dinner.

"Ding ding."

A bell sounded to let Patty know that someone was at their tiny drive-through window.

"Hang on there fellas and let me get this. I'll be right back."

"No worries, Patty," John replied, "It might take us a minute to decide what we want. Right fellas?"

Trucker nodded. John looked up at the large white board on the opposite wall. It was filled with little black plastic letters stuck into horizontal grooves, spelling out the items on the menu.

"Oh boy, that Chicken Fried Steak sure looks good." The big man smacked his lips. "Dumplin' won't let me eat that when she's with me. Says it's gonna clog my arteries. At my age, who cares if your arteries are clogged? Every meal could be your last anyway. Ain't that right?"

Long John agreed, but Trucker was busy eyeing Henry Fisher, who had, years earlier, chased him out of Babe Honeycutt's pickup with a broom. Trucker was still holding a grudge.

"Hey Henry." John had followed Truckers glare to see who was on the receiving end, "What ya doing here tonight? Where's L.D.?"

Henry got up from a bright orange upholstered booth, and went to shake John's hand.

"Aw, my Little Darlin' is over at Mrs. Belle's with her quilting group. Told me I was on my own tonight for supper."

Henry looked at Long John and nodded, then looked and Trucker and semi-scowled.

"Trucker," he warily acknowledged, hoping that by doing so, he would thwart any misbehavior by the ornery little cuss.

Big John interrupted the scowling competition between the two men. He motioned for his friend to sit down.

"Well that's exactly what I'm doin' here too. Ya wanna join us?"

"Nah," Henry waved the invitation away, "I'm already done eatin', and I need ta go next door and inventory some fan belts that came in today."

"Alright, next time then."

John stood up and shook Henry's hand again, then slapped him on the back.

"You holler when those gals of ours leave us as bachelors, and we'll grub up together."

"Will do," Henry agreed. "Long John; Trucker." He nodded as he turned to go.

"Errrrr," Trucker growled in return.

John Davis looked at Trucker, trying to assess the hostility.

"Trucker, what's your problem with Henry? He's a darn good fellow."

"Er err er errr errrr errrr er," Trucker hissed.

John looked to Long John.

"You duddn't wanna git en ta it," he warned. "Let's jest say it involved a broom, en leave it thur."

Patty ran back to the table.

"It's busier in here than a brothel on half-price night," she exhaled. "What'll it be boys?"

"Well if ya promise not to tell Dumplin' on me, I'm gonna have the Chicken Fry." John sheepishly grinned.

"If I told the things I learned in this place," Patty laughed, "I'd right well own this town. Gravy on that?"

"Wouldn't have it any other way." John smiled.

"Okay boys, you're up." Patty waited for Long John and Trucker's order.

"Trucker errred and Long John agreed. "Morty burgers en strawberry malts."

"Both of ya?" Patty hesitated, not knowing if Trucker was on board. Like every other store owner in town, she had had a first row seat to Trucker's antics in the past.

Any time that Long John had been under the weather, Trucker was forced to venture out alone. When Patty waited on him, because she couldn't understand his gibberish, she would just end up bringing him whatever he had ordered the previous time he had come in.

She was usually wrong, which would lead to Trucker throwing the order at her, leaving her covered in grease, catsup and mustard.

Long John responded to her question. "Yep, both of us."

Trucker nodded and erred.

"Okay, you fellas hang tight and we'll have it out to ya in two shakes of a gnat's wings."

Patty hollered to her sister as she left the table.

"Two Mortys and a Golden Steak Special. Sauce it up!"

John Davis, Long John, and Trucker, chitchatted until their food arrived. Then the conversation completely ceased while they hungrily wolfed down the burgers and steak.

"Boys, it just doesn't get any better than that." John rubbed his belly. "Don't tell Dumplin' I said that," he leaned over and whispered to his guests. "Now don't you get me wrong, that woman can cook, but ever since I started to have heart problems, she makes me eat like a rabbit. Ain't no sense in livin' a hundred years if you can't put gravy on it."

Long John and Trucker agreed. John Davis took the greasy, paper check that Patty had left on their table, and went to the cash register by the front door. After he paid he looked back at the Tinsleys.

"You boys ready to get in the truck, and head back to the home?"

Trucker let out an enthusiastic "Er er," to which Long John deciphered as a "Yes sir!"

Their chauffer settled into the driver's seat, while Long John lankily climbed up the tail gate, and into the bed of the truck. Then he extended his arm to Trucker so he could help the miniature and very full man up and over the gate. Trucker's right leg could barely touch the bed as he straddled the tailgate. Finally, with Long John pulling on him, and Trucker grunting loudly, he swung his left stubby limb over, and went straight to the wheel well. He took a seat and grinned.

"You boys in?" John called back to them.

"Errr!" Trucker beamed.

"Yeah!" Long John reported.

The old truck fired up and began moving. Gravel crunched under the semi-balding tires. The still warm early September air caressed Trucker's face as he leaned his head over the side of the truck in direct line with the current.

THE TINSLEYS

Long John had never seen Trucker smile like he did when he was in the back of a pickup truck. He couldn't have been happier if he were a dog.

Chapter Twelve

L ater that evening as Daphney, Ponder, and Lorelei, were in the playroom watching *Happy Days*, Trucker walked in and stood in front of the television, blocking their view. Long John stood next to him with his hands clasped in front of him.

"Err errr err err errrr," Trucker announced.

Others, who were watching the show, began caterwauling for the two men to get out of the way. Their protests prevented Long John from issuing his report—which was that Trucker said it was time for their meeting.

Trucker, upset not only with the ruckus, but the fact that his posse wouldn't listen, turned to find something he could throw at them. He quickly spotted a plastic vase, which also contained plastic flowers, on top of the television. He grabbed it, heaved it over his head, and let it fly.

Lorelei jumped out of the way, just as went careening into the crowd of Tinsleys.

"That's just enough of that!"

Mrs. James, one of the very few elderly residents at the home, rose from her seat and shook her finger at Trucker. For some reason, Mrs. James had more of a hold on the obstinate, undersized man, than anyone ever had. Trucker bowed his head and stepped back.

"Er errrr," he apologized.

Long John had not figured out how this woman—who had only been a resident for a couple of years—had managed to so easily control his almost uncontrollable friend. But, from the moment she had moved into the home, her word was law.

Her first day there, the eighty-year-old woman explored the facility. It was then that she had come across Trucker and Long John sitting in the floor of their room. They were making machine gun sounds while playing with plastic army men.

The blue-haired lady stopped at their door, and silently watched them. Long John noticed her first. He glanced up and waved to her. She smiled at him.

Trucker, deeply involved in his military escapades, hadn't noticed the exchange, and continued playing.

The woman sought Trucker's attention.

"Well who do we have here?" she asked Long John.

Only when Long John answered her, did Trucker stop playing in order to look up. When he did, he gasped, and jumped to his feet. He walked over to her and examined her, from her shoes all the way to her hair.

"Er," he shyly said.

Long John translated for him. "He said hi."

"Well hello to you, young man." She warmly smiled. "What's your name?"

Trucker looked a little surprised—even taken aback—at the question, but he quickly answered.

"Er's er—Errrrr."

"Itsa me, Harold," Long John retold.

"Hello Harold." Mrs. James seemed genuinely happy to meet him.

"Er," he replied, bashfully kicking the sole of his shoe on the floor.

"Hi," Long John passed on.

"Are you boys having a good time?" Mrs. James, pointed to the army men on the floor.

Trucker smiled a large and silly grin.

"Er er," he shyly returned.

"Uh huh," Long John concurred.

"Splendid!" The woman clasped her hands. "Well I hope to see you both again soon."

When she turned to leave the room, Trucker lunged, trying to halt her. He grabbed the back of her blue and pink flowered dress.

Startled, Mrs. James turned back to face Trucker.

"Oh my! That's not a nice thing to do young man," she scolded him.

Trucker's eyes bulged in horror, when he realized he had grabbed her. He took a step backward, obviously ashamed.

"Er errrr," he humbly apologized. "Er errrr," he said again, while looking extremely sorrowful.

"He's sorry," Long John reported. "He's sorry."

Mrs. James could see that she had scared the chubby man, leaving him a little wrecked, and vulnerable. She immediately felt sorry for him, and apologized in return.

"I'm the one who is sorry. I didn't mean to scare you." She walked over to Trucker and put her hand on his prickly cheek. "You're really a dear boy aren't you?"

Trucker bit his lower lip, and then smiled, showing her his partially toothless grin.

She laughed. "Oh you're a little devil," she teased.

Trucker, kicked non-existent dirt on the floor, and erred almost as if purring. Mrs. James patted his head.

"Okay boys, I'm going to be getting along now. You have fun with your army men."

She turned and left the room.

Long John tilted his head, trying to size up what had just happened. In all the years he had known his friend, he had never—never—seen an exchange like that between Trucker and another human being. It was as if Mrs. James had him transfixed. It almost seemed as if he had a deep and profound love for her already. It was the kind of exchange between a son and his long lost mother. Long John was stunned.

Trucker was still staring at the door where the old woman had exited, his hands down to his sides and his body swaying from side to side. It wasn't until Long John cleared his throat that Trucker's trance was broken.

"Err's errr," Trucker wistfully sighed.

"She's here?" Long John echoed.

Trucker shook his head up and down, and told Long John, "Finally."

Trucker made it a habit from that day on to go and see Mrs. James. Sometimes, he and Long John would eat lunch with her. She tolerated their mischievousness for the most part, but she was not shy about scolding them. Trucker always straightened up and behaved as soon as she did. Long John really didn't have to because he was usually not the one misbehaving in the first place.

It amazed Long John the power the old woman held over his companion. It was truly as if, the lady was Trucker's mother. Long John had never seen him so well behaved as when she was around.

>o<

"Trucker you pick that mess up off the floor and then you apologize to everyone here," Mrs. James ordered him.

Trucker looked mortified that he was going to have to apologize to his minions, but he unwillingly did so.

"Er errrr," he half-heartedly hmphed.

Long John saw his chance to explain the reason for Trucker's interruption, and he did so.

"We's needs ta have a meetin'," he told Lorelei, Ponder and Daphney. "Come on ta our room."

He motioned for them to follow him.

Ponder began to slowly rise but Lorelei was mad, and she put her hands on her hips and refused.

"I ain't goin!'" She stuck her chin haughtily in the air. "Trucker ain't my boss. I'm watchin' *Happy Days*. I don't care what ya'll say."

"Suit yerself." Long John shrugged, and turned to leave.

Seeing that her grandstanding had not earned her the respect she wanted, Lorelei quickly caved.

"Hey wait for me!"

She climbed over the chairs in front of her and followed the small group—including the chastised ring leader—out the door.

Chapter Thirteen

After Long John had fetched Maybelline and brought her to their room, the meeting began. Trucker sat down on the floor and the rest followed his lead—all except for Long John, who was finding it increasingly harder to get his long legs coiled under him because of arthritis. Instead, he took a seat on his bed. Trucker started to object, but when Long John pointed to his legs, Trucker obliged him the more comfy seating.

"Err err er errr," Trucker announced. "Er're errrr errr Err Errr."

He stood in front of at his followers, with a gigantic grin plastered across his face, waiting to gage their reactions.

Long John looked a little startled at the pronouncement, even hesitating before telling the others, until Trucker erred at him.

"Trucker's got an idea?" His voice revealed his puzzlement. "We'rea gonna find Old Pete."

The four remaining Tinsleys gasped.

"Old Pete?" Maybelline's eyes grew wide.

"We're gonna find Old Pete?" Lorelei cocked her head.

Trucker was pleased with the shock his announcement had brought. That is until Lorelei took the wind out of his sails.

"I didn't knows he was lost. Daphney and I just saw him this morning walking past the fence."

"ER!" Trucker shook his head.

"Err er err. Er'er errrr errr err errrr."

"No, we're gonna find his house." Long John replayed.

Ponder scratched his head, thinking about Trucker's plan.

Daphney scowled before whispering, "Snakes."

"Er," Trucker shook his head. "Errrr errrrrrrrrr."

"They's hibernatin'," Long John parroted, before he looked at the rest of them. Then he shrugged. "Its might be fun."

Ponder continued scratching his head.

"Old…Pete…lives…in…da…woods."

"Scary," Daphney shivered.

"What if we get lost?" Lorelei questioned.

"Er errrrr errrrrr er err," Trucker informed her.

"He's already figured thet out," Long John said.

"How?" Lorelei demanded.

Trucker nodded for Long John to explain.

"We's got supplies."

Maybelline wasn't convinced.

"What kinda supplies?"

"Errr!"

Trucker was getting annoyed that the rest of his entourage wasn't blindly following his brilliant dictate.

"Stuff," said Long John.

In light of the news, Ponder stopped scratching his head. Then he somberly agreed.

"Yeah…it…might…bea…fun."

Maybelline bit her lower lip and looked at Daphney.

Daphney took her index finger and tapped her cheek acting as if she was in deep thought.

"Hmmm, let my see."

Although she wanted to pretend that she was as wary as the others, Lorelei found it hard to contain her excitement. Her tapping foot, and quivering legs gave her away. When she could no longer contain herself she revealed her true feelings.

"I think we should do it! We gotta do it! It's the bestest thing we could ever do! We HAVE to do it!"

Each Tinsley looked at the others, then heads began bobbing in agreement, and smiles broke out all around— except, of course for Ponder, who remained stoic.

"Errrrr errr." Trucker sheepishly grinned.

"Tanight then," Long John announced.

The girls began whispering and giggling amongst themselves. Ponder calmly stared straight ahead, adding nothing to the remaining session. In short order, the group broke apart to go their separate ways, and contemplate their greatest and scariest escapade yet.

>○<

Ponder sat on his bed wondering if he and his friends may have bitten off more than they could chew. He had been through a lot of scary things in his fifty-four years of life and the one thing he knew, was that he didn't like going through scary things.

He thought back to the time when he was just a boy and a group of men in white sheets, holding fire torches, had come to his house.

He remembered getting out of bed, and looking out the window when he heard his father yelling into the deep night.

Ponder's family had been living in a place called Louisiana at the time. At first, he saw the fire and thought that the tree in the front yard was burning. But, when he rubbed the sleep from his eyes, he began to see the silhouettes, which emerged from the darkness surrounding their small share cropping farm.

He heard his pa cock the shotgun that he kept by the front door, and then heard his mother screaming for her husband to stay inside.

His father, however, paid her no attention. Instead, he bravely swung open the rickety wooden door. He stepped out onto the porch, to face the hooded gang.

"Boy," he heard a voice from the darkness yell, "you best put that gun down or you're gonna be in worse trouble than you already are!"

"Well, I don't think that I'm the one about to be in trouble," he father calmly replied. He raised the gun to his eye.

Ponder saw the white hooded heads in the group look at each other. One started to back away.

"We're coming back for you boy!" the ring leader finally lamented. "This ain't over!"

Ponder, for the first time in his life, felt his heart pound out of his chest. He didn't know why he had been so terrified. Maybe it was because he had never before heard his mother sob. Maybe it was his father's own ashen appearance when he returned from the porch. Or maybe it was the ghost like appearances of the men in his front yard.

Whatever it was, he knew at his core he had just come face to face with evil, and no matter what his conscious mind made of the event, his heart had been forever seared with the knowledge that there were things in the world that should make one very, very, afraid.

It wasn't long after that event that Ponder and his family left Louisiana. His memory of that time was somewhat fuzzy, but he did recall hearing his parents talk about starting over near their relatives in Konawa, Oklahoma. He heard them say that things were better there. He didn't know what that meant, or even if it was true, but he did know that no sheet cloaked men had ever come to their new place south of the small town.

In his entire lifetime, Ponder had never felt unloved. He knew he was different, but other than allowing him extra time to get things done, his mother and father treated him as if he had no handicap. And although he had never gone to school like other kids, and he had never had a job like adults, he was no stranger to hard work.

When Ponder was only fifteen, his pa announced that they were no longer able to make ends meet from just selling their home grown vegetables, eggs, and pork. He told his wife and son that he would be taking on a fulltime job at the plastic cup factory in Maiden. Ponder went from being his father's assistant, to taking care of almost everything on their small farm.

He didn't mind though. It provided him with a sense of accomplishment. It was as if he had become a real adult.

He quickly realized he was good at it too, and the transition was seamless. He put in long hours and would go home bone tired but that just made him proud of himself.

Many nights, long after the sun had set, Ponder's father would find him still in the barn. For a few moments, he would stand in the shadows watching the young man while he distributed hay or cleaned a stall. He would then walk to his side and wrap an arm around Ponder's muscular shoulder.

"It'll be there tomorrow Ponder," his pa would say. "You need to get some sleep so you can do it all again."

Ponder would reluctantly follow his father inside, but only after taking a moment to look around and admire what he had already accomplished.

≻○≺

Ponder sighed. He missed those days of feeling responsible and needed. He almost missed them as much as he missed his ma and pa.

The man had only come to Tinsley's a few years previously, after both his parents and several of his aunties and uncles had passed away. Of the remaining family members, there was really no one who could care for him—although his favorite cousin, Beulah, had tried for a couple of years.

Beulah had her own children, and was a kindergarten teacher, but she did what she could to help keep Ponder in groceries. She taught him how to keep his house tidy and how to cook simple things. But it became apparent—when he almost burned down the homestead by leaving a TV dinner in the oven too long—that he needed someone with him all the time.

The following day, Beulah sat him down and told him she was scared that he might end up hurting himself or worse. She asked him if he would consider living at Tinsley's.

At first Ponder was scared, but Beulah reassured him that she would see him just as much—if not more than she already did. She also told him that he would be able to make friends there. He liked the idea of actually having friends for the first time in his life, so he agreed.

Beulah had been right. Ponder hadn't realized how lonely he had been until he began forming the friendships he had with Trucker, Long John, Lorelei, Daphney and Maybelline. They had become like family to him, and he couldn't bring himself to imagine his life without them.

Beulah was true to her word too. She came regularly bearing gifts of her wonderful home cooking—even enough for his friends. She also brought him clothing and his very favorite thing—story books.

Beulah had been the one who had taught him his ABC's and had even managed to help him read the same books as the first and second graders. Almost every time she brought him a new book, she would sit with him and help him with the big words. But over the years, he had gotten very good at reading and many times, he didn't need her help at all.

While at Tinsley's, two things consistently reminded him of home, and they were both on the television.

One of Ponder's favorite memories was watching *The Lawrence Welk Show* with both his parents. It aired on the

Oklahoma Public Television Station—one of only three stations they could get.

Ponder loved music. It had been a part of his life for as long as he could remember. Even though his family never had a lot, his mother had a wonderful table top Victor Victrola which had been handed down to her by her own mother. Endless evenings had been spent listening to the enchanting sounds that came through its big horn.

Ponder especially loved The Rice Brother's Gang's *You Are My Sunshine*. Even though it hadn't been released until he was 17, once his mother discovered his love for it, she would sing it to him every night before he went to bed.

Ponder would get lost in all the music they listened to, as he watched his father and mother dance and sway to the melodies coming from the gramophone. When he moved into Tinsley's, there was not enough room for the large machine, so Beulah had kept it for him.

Being without it was by far the hardest part of living at the home. But being able to watch Lawrence Welk ever Saturday night, with all his crooners and dancers, was a small piece of heaven for him.

The other thing he liked to watch was *The CBS Evening News with Walter Cronkite*. Every weekday night, while his mother was preparing supper, he and his father would settle in and watch the stories being told by the man with a small graying mustache.

He particularly remembered seeing stories about something called Watergate (although he had never figured out what that was), and a war involving Americans that was taking place in a hot, wet place in the jungle.

He asked his pa where the place was, and he was told Vee it name. Since that time—although he didn't like all the explosions he saw—he did wish to see the jungles of Vee for himself.

That idea became cemented when the television series *Tarzan* came out in 1966. He never missed an episode in its two year run.

Then, as if Heaven had descended upon him, his mother took him to see *The Jungle Book* at The Majestic Theater in Maiden. It was the one and only time he had ever gotten to go to the picture show.

While the movie was animated, the colors of the jungle with all its animals, brought a whole new infatuation. The black and white pictures from their old TV set, couldn't hold a candle to the rich, and magical beauty that had unfolded before his eyes. It was the most exciting thing Ponder had ever seen, and he decided right then and there, that if he could go anywhere in the entire world, it would be to the jungle.

It was only a few short months later that Walter Cronkite actually relayed his stories about the war, from Vee. Ponder remembered being horribly jealous.

He turned to his father and asked if they could go too. His father looked over at his only son.

"That's the last place on earth you want to be boy," he had said.

Ponder couldn't understand why, but the look on his pa's face told him he should not bring it up again. Instead, he'd day dream about a time in the future, when he could wear a safari hat, and enter into the thick, dark green foliage. He would befriend a panther like Bagheera, and maybe—like Tarzan— even swing from the vines with monkeys.

Ponder was surprised when even after moving into Tinsley's, Walter Cronkite had continued to tell stories and show pictures of Vee. He would sit in the TV room, watch and pretend that his father was right beside him, and that his mother was busy preparing their supper.

It was only in the past year, that Ponder heard the newsman say the war was over. The old people around him clapped. He wasn't sure why they were clapping, but he joined them anyway.

What they didn't see, was that there were tears sliding down Ponder's cheeks. The very thing that had them celebrating, was instead making his heart hurt. He knew that not seeing Vee nightly would mean that the last thing he had left that connected him to his father and to the jungle, was gone for good.

The loss of that connection was one of the reasons Ponder had agreed to that night's adventure. The woods where Old Pete lived, reminded him of the pictures he had seen of the heavily vegetative areas of Vee. He was still a little apprehensive, but there was an excitement tingling inside him too. This adventure would probably be the closest he would ever get to a real jungle.

He crawled under his covers and slowly drifted to sleep, all the while imagining the amazing things he might see in the coming hours.

Chapter Fourteen

It felt as if Ponder had barely just fallen asleep when the familiar erring awoke him.

"Err Er," Trucker nudged him.

"Git up," Long John echoed.

"Is…it…already…time…to…go?" Ponder sleepily sat up and blinked at the two.

"Soon as we's gits tha girls," Long John answered.

Ponder got out of bed, and slipped into his brown leather house shoes. Since they were going to the jungle, he thought that maybe he should wear his real shoes, but when he mentioned it, Trucker growled at him.

"Let's go en git tha others." Long John motioned for the two to follow him. They snuck down the hall, and into Lorelei and Daphney's room.

"Err er," Trucker repeated his previous orders to Ponder.

Lorelei rolled over and sat up so quickly it scared the three men.

"Yay!" she loudly whispered. "I been waitin', and waitin', and waitin', for ya'll." She jumped out of bed and hurriedly put on her slippers. Then she went to Daphney's bed and jumped up and down on it.

"Daphney! Get up, get up, get up!" It's time to go find Old Pete's house."

Daphney responded with a moan, and tried to slap her roommate away.

"Daaaaaaaaaph Neeeeeeee," Lorelei stopped jumping and instead bent over, placing her face mere inches from her sleepy friend.

"You have to get up. We're going to find Old Pete. We're goin' right now." She shoved Daphney, who still refused to wake up.

Lorelei got on her knees and closely examined Daphney's face. She blew on it, and waited. Daphney just moaned. She raised one of Daphney's eyelids and peered into her eye. Then she dropped the lid and turned to the rest of the group.

"I don't think she's getting' up." She shrugged and then climbed off the bed.

"Errrr err errr."

"We gonna leave er den," Long John disclosed.

As quickly as Lorelei had jumped out of bed, Daphney did too.

"Not leave!" She stamped her foot. "Not leave!"

"Ummmmm," Lorelei pointed to the now energized woman. "You was fakin'. Faker!"

Daphney grinned wide, then shyly lowered her head, only minutely ashamed of herself.

"Errr er!"

Trucker's irritation could be easily heard amidst his undecipherable dialogue, so Daphney quickly dressed in her robe and slipped on her shoes.

"Go en git Maybelline," Long John pointed to Lorelei.

"You guys wait on me," Lorelei ordered when she had gotten down on her hands and knees to crawl down the hall. "Don't you dare leave."

As soon as Maybelline and Lorelei had safely crawled back past the nurses' station, the band slowly, and quietly, made their way to the exit door. Just as Trucker started to open it, Long John grabbed him. Trucker briskly turned around and scowled.

"We's forgot tha supplies." Long John held out his empty hands.

Trucker let out a little, but agitated growl, before pushing Long John back toward their room.

The rest of the group waited anxiously, staring down the hall to watch, not only for their comrades, but also, any nurses or aides that might spoil their get-away.

When Trucker and Long John returned with rope, glue, and some biscuits they had swiped from the cafeteria, the posse all tried exiting the door at the same time.

"Err err er err err!" Trucker swatted at the congregation.

Long John agreed, "Git outta tha way."

He stuck his long arm in front of the group blocking them so that he and Trucker could leave first. The rest followed, but not before Long John scolded Lorelei for giggling out loud.

When they were all safely outside, and the door was silently closed, Trucker again took charge.

"Errrrr er er!" he ordered.

Long John pointed to Trucker. "Listen to em," he authoritatively directed.

Trucker outlined in detail, that the group was going to cross North Street—the one they had already walked many times on their outings—and then sneak across the field, and into the woods.

"Not...da...woods." Ponder slowly shook his head. "It's...a...jungle."

"Snakes," Daphney whispered.

Trucker erred at Daphney, and raised an eyebrow at Ponder, but quickly commenced dictating the rest of the plan.

He pointed directly north and informed his followers that Old Pete's house was located over mountains, rivers, and after hearing Ponder's pronouncement, through the jungle. Everyone's eyes grew wide. Lorelei clapped her hands in excitement although Daphney bit her lip.

"Err's er," he motioned for the assembly to follow him.

"Let's go," Long John agreed.

The pajama clad troop headed across North Street and walked the hundred yards toward the woods. Lorelei was skipping as Daphney clung to Maybelline's robe sleeve. Ponder wondered aloud about Trucker's plan for safe passage.

"How…we…gonna…git…over…da…river?" he asked.

Trucker pointed to the rope that Long John carried.

"Hmmm…," Ponder replied. "I…can't…walk…no… tightrope. My…feets…are…too…big."

He stopped to look down at his large house slippers, and then pointed to them for the rest of the group to see.

"Err't errrerrr errrerr'," Trucker shook his head.

"Ain't tightrope walkin'," Long John imparted, although he wasn't sure what tightrope walking was.

The answer seemed to satisfy Ponder's curiosity, and he silently continued trudging along, until the gang had reached the edge of the woods.

Trucker turned around quickly to face the ensemble. "Er's errrr er errerrerrr er errr er er errr er err," he instructed.

Long John pointed at the Tinsleys.

162

"Itsa gonna be dangerous in thur so doos what he says."

Daphney released Maybelline's arm, and began to back away. "Not go." She shook her head.

"Daphney!" Lorelei stomped her foot, "You gotta go. You can't stay here."

She reached out her arms to show Daphney the darkness which surrounded them and warned her friend.

"Sumpin's gonna get you if you stay here by yourself."

Daphney let out a scared little moan, before squatting and grabbing her knees. She rocked herself back and forth, while she looked at the ground.

"Dangerous," she whispered.

"Awww Daphney," Maybelline bent down to console her, "we're not gonna let anything happen to you, you know that."

Daphney looked into Maybelline's eyes, searching for truth.

Maybelline stood up and looked at the rest.

"We're not gonna let nothin' happen to her, are we?"

Heads began shaking and although slowly, Ponder was the first to reassure her.

"No…Daphney,…we's…not…eber…gonna…let…

sumthin'…happen…to…yous."

Lorelei made a fist and showed her friend.

"That's right! I'll beat up anything that tries to hurt you!"

"We's gonna protect ya Daphney," Long John chimed in.

Trucker just sighed with impatience, but finally erred.

Daphney stood up and smoothed her robe and nightgown. "Kay," she sniffed. "I go."

Lorelei did a little jig, and Trucker motioned for everyone to fall into line once again. Then they entered the dark woods.

Chapter Fifteen

orelei didn't know why she was so excited about the night's adventure. All she knew was that she somewhat loved being a little scared. Her heart would race and she could feel it pound through her chest.

Although the time was so far removed, she couldn't really remember the reason, she could remember the first time it had happened like it was yesterday.

She was with someone she thought had to have been her mother. They had been sleeping under a large stone railroad trestle. The structure was more like a cave because one end had silted in. She had even asked the mother-woman if they were in a cave, but she was told to hush and go to sleep.

She remembered being hungry and telling the woman who then dug through a cloth sack, and pulled out some dried beef for Lorelei to suck on.

"We'll go find a hen house, and get some eggs in the morning," she was told.

Lorelei had settled into the woman's side and sucked on the meat. She was almost asleep when she heard rustling outside the cave. The woman sat up and put her hand over Lorelei's mouth, to ensure her silence. Then they both waited and listened.

The cracking of dried leaves and tall grass permeated the chamber. Lorelei remembered the lump in her throat. Then she felt it—a tha-thump, tha-thump, tha-thump right under that lump. She instinctively put her hand to her throat to touch the pulsating beat. She noticed she could feel it in her chest too. Her face was hot and she began to sweat. She didn't think she liked the feeling—or did she?

The closer the rustling sound came, the closer the woman pulled Lorelei to her. With her hand still over Lorelei's mouth, she tried to tuck the small girl behind her.

Lorelei didn't like that because she wanted to see what was going to happen next. She peeked her head around the waist that shielded her. She could feel that the woman had stopped breathing. She could also feel the pounding of the woman's own chest, beating even faster than hers, and when the sound was right upon them, for one moment, time froze,

She heard the woman exhale loudly. That's when she saw it —the silhouette of a large black dog.

A long, club like tail began to wag, and she heard the woman chuckle a little, her body releasing its sharp tenseness. Lorelei felt her own shoulders drop and the racing in her chest, begin to slow. It was then that she decided she liked the feeling because it made her feel…well, alive.

Lorelei was seven when she was abandoned by the mother-woman, at a bus station somewhere in Oklahoma. She remembered the woman placing her on a bench, and telling her to wait there. She did as she was told, and sat there for a long time. Finally, she curled up and went to sleep.

The next thing she remembered, she was being shaken by a gray-haired and mustached' man in a blue uniform. When she fully awoke, he began to ask her a lot of questions, like who she was; who was with her; and where were they going?

Lorelei was very nervous because she didn't know the answers. She blinked her eyes and looked around, searching for the woman who could answer them. She didn't see her anywhere, so she just shrugged her shoulders.

The man in the uniform didn't seem to mind that she didn't know. He took her by the hand and brought her to a small office. He gave her a sandwich and a bottle of orange soda. She devoured the sandwich and swallowed the pop in gulps. She didn't remember ever having anything as good. She thought that maybe she hadn't eaten in a long time.

To that day, the memory of the food often sent her into town, where she made a stop at Stephen's Drugstore for an orange soda, and Ralph's Grocery for a baloney and cheese sandwich. Each bite would take her back to that bus station and the nice man who had fed her.

After she ate, the man sat her on top of a grey metal desk and began to ask her more questions. There was only one that she was able to answer. Lorelei—her name was Lorelei.

It was just a short time before two policemen came into the office and spoke with the man. They asked him a lot of questions too, and it made Lorelei feel better, because he didn't know the answers either.

The men spoke softly to her. One pulled off his black jacket and wrapped it around her. It almost went to the floor. Then they took her to their car and put her in the backseat. One of the men sat there with her as they rode to the station.

Once there, they took her into another office, and offered her a Mallo Cup. She shyly bit into it. The milk chocolate and marshmallow center whisked her away to a place of bliss she had never known. Like the soda and sandwich, it remained one of her favorite treats.

Later on, Lorelei had been taken to a house, and for the first time that she could ever remember, she slept in a bed. She remained at that place only a few days, before she was put into a home, with a lot of other girls. She remembered cots lined up in a big hollow room with a cement floor. It seemed as if there were hundreds of them.

She often wondered what happened to the mother-woman, but she never saw her again. She heard grownups talk about things like custody and abandonment. She heard them talk of a court, and a judge, but she didn't know what any of it meant.

She didn't remember being lonely. She actually liked having a bed and food in her stomach. She also didn't mind that she didn't have any friends, especially since most of the girls were mean. It was at that place that Lorelei had learned she had to be tough.

On her second day there, a girl named Anita shoved her while she was standing in line to get her lunch. At first, Lorelei thought it was an accident, but when the other girls started yelling at Anita to hit her, Lorelei, in a panic, shoved her back. She pushed her so hard, the girl went careening across the floor, stopping at the feet of a sour looking woman. The woman pulled Anita up by her collar, and marched her back into line with a stern warning.

"Keep it up and you'll regret it."

All eyes had been on Lorelei that day, and although some girls made comments about her being dumb, and simple, no one ever got near enough again to her to touch her.

Lorelei was eighteen when she'd gone to Tinsley's. The woman from the girl's home, had brought her into a room with peeling blue wallpaper, and told her she couldn't stay there anymore. She said Lorelei she was too old, and had aged out. She wasn't sure what that meant.

Like Maybelline, Lorelei didn't know her actual birthdate, but she had known she was seven the year she was found. So on the first of January 1962, she was transported to Tinsleys.

She remembered how cold it had been that day, and she was extra-glad that she had been given a big brown and tan coat to keep her warm.

It wasn't often during the ensuing years that she ever got to feel the rush that she had felt the night she saw the dog—that is until Trucker had found they could sneak out.

Every single time she was awakened to go on one of their adventures, she would begin to feel the joyful rush. It was even more pronounced if they came close to being discovered, either by making too much noise or by accidently leaving clues that they had been out. As far as she was concerned, it was one of the best feelings ever.

≻o≺

As the small party stepped into the dark woods, Lorelei felt the familiar charge course through her veins. It almost made her giddy.

"Ohhhh, dark." Daphney ducked behind her, clinging to the back of her gown.

"Yeah!" Lorelei was delighted.

"Errrr!" Trucker turned around, and gruffly pointed to them.

"Shhhh!" Long John said.

Trucker leaned in to discuss something with Long John, as Ponder tried to get his eyes to adjust to the jungle they had entered.

"Trucker says we's gotta be quiet so's thet he kin listen fer Old Pete," Long John reported.

Everyone froze and remained silent for several minutes, until Trucker pointed straight ahead of them, and motioned for the motley crew to continue. The Tinsleys traipsed for several moments, before Maybelline got her gown caught on a wild Blackberry bush. It stopped her in her tracks.

"I'm stuck. I can't get loose!" she cried out.

Trucker erred some profanities.

"I help."

Daphney leaned down to get a closer look at the entanglement, and then pulled on the caught material.

A small ripping sound penetrated the night.

"Awwww, Daphney you broke it!" Maybelline chastised her friend.

"Not break."

Daphney stood and held up a torn but loose piece of gown.

"Fixed," she pointed to Maybelline, who was now free from the thorny plant.

"Oh you did," Maybelline agreed. "I ain't stuck anymore."

Trucker erred at his followers to continue, so they did. The pilgrimage was slow going however, as fallen trees, Bull Nettle plants, and the already conquered wild Blackberry bushes, were more than abundant in the ever more dense timber.

The further they went, the more frustrated Trucker became. He turned and warned Ponder.

"E'r errrr er errrerr er err!"

Long John pointed to Ponder.

"He's tired of watin' on ya!"

Trucker had a point. The normally slow man had also become a purposeful one. He often stopped to investigate hanging vines, cedar seedlings, and any other odd thing that caught his eye.

The others took their cue and started complaining too.

"When we gonna get there?" Lorelei whined.

"Tired," Daphney sighed.

"We been in here hours," Maybelline hmphed, although it had really been about twenty minutes.

"Errrrr, err errer er. Err errrr er err, errr err'er errers." Trucker irately scolded. "Er're ererrr errrr."

Long John recounted Truckers admonishment.

"Ponder, yous hurry up. Tha rest of yas, hold yer horses; we're almost thur."

It was true, they could have almost been to Old Pete's place, but they had crossed the field and entered the woods at least one hundred yards west of his shack. And even though they were almost even with it at that point, there was no way they could see it through the thicket and darkness.

Trucker put his arms out to stop his followers.

"Errrer Errrr." He pointed in front of him.

"Jumper Crick," Long John disclosed.

"Ohhhhh." Daphney backed up a step.

"Yay!" screamed Lorelei. "Jumper Creek!"

Ponder, the last to arrive, looked at the small creek.

"How's…we…gonna…gets…across…without… gettin'…wet?" he laggardly asked Trucker.

Trucker beamed like he was the king of everything. He pointed to the rope, and pulled out the tube of Liquid Nails.

"Errr errr."

"With this." Long John held up the rope for everyone to see.

"Ahhhhhhh," the group responded in unison—even though they were completely clueless as to its use.

Trucker began looking skyward in search of a large tree from which to hang the rope. After much scanning, he couldn't find one big enough to hold them. Trucker emanated his displeasure with a growl, then motioned for his groupies to follow him downstream.

The little underlings followed as instructed, until Maybelline lost her footing and stepped into ankle deep mud on the side of the creek.

"It's got me! It's got me!" she screamed.

Both Daphney and Lorelei jumped back screaming too, and for the second time that night, Daphney bent down, put her head between her knees, and began rocking herself.

Trucker, startled as well, swung around so quickly he knocked Long John off balance. Long John also found his own foot encased in the cold, slimy earth. He looked up at Trucker.

"Mud. Itsa jest mud."

Trucker rolled his eyes, and sighed heavily. "Err er Errererrr. Er's errr err."

Before Long John could relay Trucker's message, Maybelline—clearly hearing the disdain in Trucker's tone— brushed him off.

"I know, I know, it's only mud." She pulled her feet out of the dark mess, leaving one house shoe stuck.

Long John bent over to retrieve the wedged shoe, before joining her on dry land.

Ponder, who arrived panting, finally caught up with the group and was unaware of the mud goblin.

"Why…didda…Maybelline…scream?
I's…ran…all…da… way… here."

"It's okay. She just stepped in mud," Lorelei reported.

Daphney had returned to her upright position, but was still unsure of their safety.

"Mud," she muttered, while peering out from behind Lorelei to see if they were really out of danger.

Ponder wiped his sweaty brow.

"Dat'sa…good…thing…cause…I…thoughts…it…

mighta…been…a…tiger."

Daphney whimpered, and slid even further behind Lorelei.

"No tiger." She shook her head.

"Now look what ya did Ponder," Lorelei rebuked him.

"I's…sorry." He bowed his head, then spoke quietly to himself. "Ain't…my…fault… dat…jungles…gots…tigers."

Chapter Sixteen

Trucker again scanned the night sky above them for a tree with a good limb. It was only about ten feet away and he pointed to it.

"Errrr! Errr's errr er're errrerr err."

"Thet's what we's lookin' fer," Long John pointed as well.

Trucker told Long John to unwrap the rope from the cellophane and hand it over. When he did, Trucker took the heavy cordage and walked back a few feet. When he had uncoiled about twenty feet of it, he stepped back to examine the tree again. It took several moments for him to develop a plan and Lorelei became impatient.

"Whatcha doin?" she whined. "Let's go and find Old Pete."

She turned and smiled at Maybelline and Daphney. "He's gonna be so happy to see us!"

Daphney half-heartedly returned the smile.

"Errr err'er ererr errrer'." Trucker twirled around and pointed to her. "E'r errer' er errerrr errr err!"

"Stop yer belly achin'. He's tryin' to figure this out." Long John scowled on Trucker's behalf.

"Awww man," Lorelei sighed, and kicked the dirt. "I want him to hurry up."

Finally, Trucker took the rope, walked about five feet back, then he heaved the end of it as high and as hard he could. The rope only made it halfway to the limb.

Trucker cursed. He backed up a few more feet and tried again. This time, he managed to increase the rope's height by a couple of feet. He stomped his feet and danced in a circle, pulling at his non-existent hair. Then he let out a frustrated scream.

"ARRRRRRERRRRARRRRERRRR!"

When his tantrum was over, he turned and handed Long John the rope.

Long John took his place beside Trucker, and mimicked the previous attempts. The rope hit the side of the limb then slid off and back to earth.

"Errr er!"

"Damn it," Long John almost silently repeated.

Trucker told him to try again, and Long John obliged. This time, the rope made it over, but only by a couple of feet.

The two stood looking up at it, realizing they still needed it to drop about fifteen feet before they could reach it.

"ARRRRERRRRRRRR!" Trucker yelled again, in his frustration.

Long John pulled the rope back down, and scrunched his forehead in thought.

"Iffin we puts something heavy on it, it'll pull it down."

Trucker thought a second.

"Errr!"

With Trucker's agreement, Long John began looking around for the something heavy. He saw a volleyball sized stone at the edge of the creek and retrieved it. Then he tied the end of the rope around it, just like he tied his shoes. When he went to throw it, it only lifted a foot before it came tumbling down, and almost landing on Trucker's foot. It also had escaped the rope.

Trucker was not amused, and sighed deeply.

Likewise, Long John sighed.

"Too heavy."

He looked around again.

In the meantime Ponder walked up with a small log.

"Dis...ill...work." He handed the limb to Long John.

Long John hesitated, not wanting to be shown up by Ponder, but Trucker erred for him to get on with it. Long John reluctantly tied the rope around its end.

"Yous...needs...to...puts...it...in...da...middle," Ponder informed him, as he stepped forward to help. "En...ya... should...tie...a...knot,...not...a...bow."

Long John did not like taking directions from Ponder, and he turned to glare at him. As he did, Trucker grabbed the rope, and handed it to Ponder. Long John quickly turned to Trucker, mouth agape.

"Hey, I wasa doin' thet," he protested.

Trucker shook his head.

Ponder slowly ambled to the log, and bent over to tie the rope. When it was finally done, he picked it up and in an effort to make peace, he handed it back to Long John.

"Yous…gonna…have…to…throws…it…cuz…I…ain't … as…strong…as…yous," he lied.

Long John smiled, and took the log from Ponder's hands. He told everyone to stand back, then he put the log between his legs. He see-sawed it back and forth.

"One, two," he counted.

"Three!" everyone joined in.

"Three," Ponder trailed.

The log lifted into the air and over the tree limb. Everyone, including Trucker, jumped and clapped when it dropped to the ground bringing the rope with it.

Long John looked at Trucker, unsure of how to proceed.

"Err er err."

"Tie its off? How?" He questioningly turned to Ponder, having already forgiven him.

Ponder walked to the log. He untied the rope from it then he lethargically walked to the coiled end. He slowly made a slipknot and pulled it tightly, making sure it was secure.

"Now…what?" he asked their testy leader.

Trucker smiled big. "Er errer errrr ererrr," he beamed.

"We gonna swing across."

Long John turned back to Trucker.

"We's gonna swing across?"

Ponder showed some excitement.

"Just…like…Tarzan…of…da…jungle." He smiled and his white teeth lit up the night.

Maybelline poked Lorelei, then pointed to Ponder.

"He smiled," she somberly stated.

"Hey look at Ponder," Lorelei relayed to the group. "Ponder's smilin'."

Long John and Trucker turned to stare at the large man. It was clear that he was genuinely happy.

"He's smilin," Long John agreed. "Ponder's a smilin'!"

In all the time Ponder had been at the home, not once had any of them ever seen him smile.

They continued looking at Ponder's massive grin, and in a few short seconds, grins began to creep across their own faces—including Trucker's.

"Ponder's smilin'," Maybelline repeated.

"Smilin'," Daphney giggled, clutching her side. Then Lorelei snorted, and before they knew it, they were all laughing hysterically.

When they finally calmed down, Trucker quickly turned somber, and told them that they needed to get back to business.

"He says we gonna each swing over tha crick one et a time. Maybelline's a goin' first."

Long John handed her the rope.

Maybelline backed away.

"Me? Why me?"

Long John looked to Trucker for the answer, but it came as a growl, so Maybelline reluctantly stepped forward.

"How am I gonna get over there?"

Trucker laid out his plan, and Long John regurgitated.

"First we's gonna put this hurr glue on yer hands, en yer gonna hang on ta tha rope. Den we's gonna grab tha rope en pull yas back hurr." He pointed behind himself. "Den we'll swing yas over ta tha other side."

Maybelline wasn't sure she liked the idea, but quickly realized she was no match for Trucker's temper. She stuck out her hands in preparation for the glue. Trucker unscrewed the cap and squeezed onto her hands.

Nothing came out.

Trucker looked at the tube and then examined the hole which should have released the contents. It was sealed with the same thin metal from which the tube was constructed.

"Err!"

He lifted the end of the tube and showed it to Long John, before letting out a string of bold and inflammatory curse words. Then, in total disgust, he loudly stomped around the "jungle" floor.

With complete rage in his eyes, he turned back to Long John. Long John backed away. Snorting like a bull, Trucker released a torrent of every rotten name he could think of to call Earl.

Long John knew better than to try and calm Trucker, so instead, he tried to distract him.

"What we's gonna do now?"

Trucker erred at the top of his lungs, angrily threw the glue on the ground, and kicked at it. Then he followed the projectile to where it landed, all the while throwing around his arms, and kicking at the ground like a crazy man.

Just as Trucker was about to stomp the guts out of the container, Ponder interrupted.

"I's...thinks...I's...can...fix...it."

He leisurely bent over and retrieved the tube.

"Err?" Trucker stopped his tirade and eyed Ponder.

"Yeah,...I's...bets...it's...one...of...dem...caps...dat...ya...has...to...poke."

Trucker squinted at the large man, thinking he might be pulling his leg.

Ponder continued his examination, not looking up to see Trucker's distrust.

"Yep,…ya…gotta…break…da…end…with…dis…here top…of…da…cap."

Trucker tilted his head and growled, sure that Ponder was making it up. Ponder finally looked up.

"Nah…Trucker,…I's…serious.   My…pa…showed… me."

He took the cap and turned it upside down, shoving the sharp point into the tube's opening. Out squirted some glue. Trucker erred inquisitively, and approached Ponder to see what he had done.

Trucker took the cap from Ponder and examined it.

"Errr," he smiled, and nodded his head. "Er ererr er!"

He playfully slapped Ponder on the arm.

"Thet *is* neat." Long John agreed.

"Err's er err," Trucker excitedly directed.

"Let's go den," Long John broadcast.

Maybelline—slouched and reluctant, hesitantly stepped forward.

Chapter Seventeen

Trucker squeezed a good amount of the white pasty glue into Maybelline's outstretched palms.

"Ewww," she crinkled her nose, "slimy."

"Err 'er ererrrer," Trucker instructed her.

Long John took Maybelline's hands and clasped them together.

"He says rub 'em together."

"Ewww," Maybelline repeated.

"Nows grab tha rope en come up hurr," Long John pointed to an area behind them.

Trucker instructed the rest of the Tinsleys to go to the same area, and get behind Maybelline to push her.

"Hold on," Long John instructed.

Ponder said his temporary goodbyes.

"See...ya...later."

"See ya later," Lorelei repeated, not understanding that the other side of the creek was only ten feet away.

"Later?" Daphney somewhat sulked. "No later. My friend," she sorrowfully whispered.

"She's jest gonna be right thur." Long John pointed to show the sad woman. Daphney clapped her approval.

"Errr er errrr," Trucker, who was again annoyed, impatiently announced.

Long John grabbed the rope along with Maybelline and pulled her back.

"On three," he informed the rest. "One, two, three!"

The five remaining Tinsleys pushed Maybelline for all they were worth. Before she could even reach the bank, she slid down onto the ground. She looked up at her crew and shrugged.

"She...didn't...go...over. Why...didn't...ya...go...over? Tarzan...goes...over."

Ponder scratched his head and thought a moment.

"Hey...I...knows...da...problem. She...didn't...yell.

Everyone looked at him, eyebrows raised.

"Yous...knows.   Tarzan...goes...'Ah-E-Ah-E-Ah!' Den... he...swings...through...da...jungle."

He looked to his friends, waiting for them to comprehend. They replied with blank stares.

He...yells. Yous...has... to...yell."

Long John's light turned on.

"Oh yeah," he agreed, "he does go OOh-E-OOh-E-Ooh."

He turned to Trucker.

"Ponder's right."

Daphney tried to practice in a quiet little voice, but it came out "E-Ah, E-Ah," like a donkey.

Ponder shook his head.

"No...Daphney...iz...like...dis."

Ponder pulled his head back to the sky, and let out a loud, shrill "Ah-E-Ah-E-Ah!" He even did it with a normal cadence, which stunned the rest of the group.

Lorelei followed Ponder's example and screeched.

"Ah-E-Ah-E-Ah!"

Long John tilted his head back and released his twang version.

"OOH-E-OOH-E-OOH!"

Trucker saw nothing to do but join in.

"Er-E-Er-E-Er!"

Maybelline pushed herself up from the ground, and brought a handful of stuck dead leaves and dirt with her.

"Let's do it again!" she said excitedly. "I can yell like Tarzan!"

The group reassembled, as Maybelline once again grabbed a hold of the rope. Her friends pulled her back.

"Okay now, on three yas yell like Tarzan," Long John instructed. "One, two, THREE!"

"AH-E-AH-E-AH!" Maybelline yelled, and fell to the ground for a second time.

"Awwww," came the unison and disappointed reply.

All eyes turned to Tucker, who just shrugged.

The band of would-be Tarzans sat down to think.

"Maybe we's kin build us a boat," Long John announced.

"Maybe we can build a bridge with sticks," Maybelline interjected.

"Maybe...we...can...just...walk...over...to...da...other side." Ponder pointed downstream.

Everyone followed his gaze to see that the creek was mostly gravel and mud, with only a little pool of water. It was also only about six foot across.

The troop jumped up, and ran toward the narrow part of the creek bed. Maybelline, caked with even more dead foliage on her hands, was the first to cross by stepping on a flat rock. She then hopped over the two foot wide pool and landed on a sandbar. Then she scrambled up the side of the elevated creek bank and turned to face the others. She grinned then waved.

Trucker stomped his foot, clearly annoyed that they did not get to use the more adventuresome rope and glue. He was last to join the others as they quickly scrambled across the narrow ravine.

Once safely on the other side, Trucker looked around. He licked his finger and put it in the air as if testing the wind direction.

"Wat yas doin'?" Long John asked.

"Errrerr err ererrerrr," he looked at Long John like he was stupid.

"Our derrection?" Long John cocked his head. "Which derrection we's goin'?"

"Errr."

"East?"

"Errr."

Long John took his cue from Trucker, and pointed to the north.

"Okay everyones, we's goin' east,"

Each Tinsley fell in line behind Trucker, and continued to follow him through the woods. It was only moments before the dense brush faded into smaller clusters, which shortly gave way to an open field.

The moon was almost directly overhead, allowing the bunch to see the reflection of a small pond, in front of a grassy knoll.

Trucker stuck out his arms abruptly to stop his crew. Then he slowly pointed to the knoll on the opposite side.

Two deer and one buck stood calmly drinking from the pond's edge. Daphney ducked in behind Lorelei, then stuck her head out to peer at the animals. Lorelei could feel her shaking.

Instinctively, everyone remained still, and silent, watching the stoic beings in front of them. The buck raised its head, and sniffed the air. He turned to the deer beside him, and snorted a warning. His companions scattered into the woods on the other side of the knoll.

Daphney screamed.

"Dogs! Hurt us!"

"They *were* big dogs," Lorelei, wide eyed, agreed. "I was really skeered they was gonna eat us!"

She whipped around to face Maybelline, and see if she had been scared too.

"I don't think those was dogs," Maybelline shook her head back and forth. "I think they was ghostises."

Daphney tucked herself back behind Lorelei, and whimpered. "Ghosties."

"Deys...wuddn't...dogs...or...ghosties," Ponder matter-of-factly stated. "Deys...was...deer."

"Nope," Long John disagreed.

"Deys...was...too. I...knows...deys...was,...cause...we ...had... 'em...at...my... Ma...en...Pa's...place."

Trucker eyed Ponder to see if he was telling the truth.

Maybelline asked, "What's a deer?"

Ponder thought for a minute. "We...had...some...dat... would...come...to...our...yard...to...get...corn. Deys...was ...friendly,...but...Deys...was...a...little...scared...of...ya."

Daphney began to venture out from behind her friend.

"What's a deer?" Maybelline asked again.

"Dey's...like..." Ponder couldn't quite find the words to describe the animals.

"Dey's...like..." he paused again, before finally coming to a conclusion.

"Dey's...like...dogs."

"Dogs!" Daphney screamed and dove behind Lorelei.

Chapter Eighteen

Ponder turned from the group and began walking toward the area where the deer had been standing. The rest of the Tinsleys blindly followed—including Trucker—whose curiosity had gotten the best of him.

"Dem…wasn't…da…kind…of…deer…dat…would…eat…corn…from…yous," Ponder informed the rest. "Dey's…wild. Took…my…momma…a…long…time…to…get…da…deer…to…not…be…so…fraid…of…us. Just…kept …throwin'…some…feed…corn…to…'em. Den…one…day …deys…came…right…up…to…da…house…beggin'…for… it."

"Really?" Lorelei asked.

"Um…hm," Ponder answered. "My…pa…didn't…much …like…it…though,…cause…he…said…we…was…wastin'

…feed…for…da…pigs. Said…deer…posed…to...be…for… eatin',…not…feedin'. Ma…didn't…pay…no…mind…to… em…though. She…just…kept…feedin'…dem…deer. Deys … finally…even…let…me…pet…'em," he fondly remembered.

"Huh uh," Long John contradicted.

"Um…hm," Pondered countered.

"You eat them?" Maybelline twisted her face in horror. "I ain't never ate no dog."

"We's…didn't…eat…'em," Ponder reassured her. "Don't …knows…why…my…pa…said…that."

When the outfit got to the place the where the deer had stood, Ponder sat down. Again, the others followed his lead. He quietly stared across the water, becoming deeply entrenched in the memories of his mother, and the animals for which she cared. He felt a tear slip down his cheek, and didn't bother to wipe it away.

Ponder had often struggled with the hollowness, that seemed to permeate his very being, since he had lost his folks. He wondered if they could still see him from Heaven. He wondered if they longed to be with him, as much as he longed to be with them.

Ponder had been going to the Mount Zion Christian Church since he was a boy. He knew of Heaven, but it wasn't from the stories he had been told at church. He had actually visited the indescribable place when he was five.

It was a steamy summer day. Ponder was hot and wanted to swim. He went into the house and told his momma. She sent the boy in search of his father.

"Go ask you daddy ta take ya down to the pond," she told the small child.

Ponder obeyed and went to the barn to get his pa. He didn't find him there, so he combed the rest of the small acreage looking for him. His search was in vain.

It was getting hotter by the minute, and that's when he decided that his daddy must already be swimming at the pond. Even though Ponder's pa had incessantly warned him to never to go alone, the child reasoned that if his father was already there, then he could be too. He headed down the back pasture and through a small thicket to join him.

When Ponder got to the water, he didn't see his father. He hollered, but got no answer. Ready to obey, he turned to leave. But then, but something caught his eye. It was his pa's head smack dab in the middle of the pond.

Ponder undressed as fast as he could, and jumped in toward his father. He dog paddled toward the head for all he was worth. His pa still had not turned around and Ponder wondered why he hadn't heard him coming. The boy decided it was better that way, because then, he could surprise him. Ponder had only gotten about twenty feet when he started to get tired.

"Pa?" he called out to the head. "Git…me. Imma… tired."

The head didn't move, which confused Ponder. Maybe his father hadn't heard him.

"Pa?!" he yelled louder. "Git… me."

Ponder's legs began to feel like lead. He wondered if he could touch the bottom. He slowly let himself sink, reaching his foot out as far as he could, trying to feel the base of the pond.

Ponder's head was completely submerged, and he wasn't touching anything. That is when he began to panic. Why didn't his father grab him? He fought his way back to the surface and gasped in a mouthful of air.

"Help... me... Pa!" he yelled before sinking again.

Ponder opened his mouth to repeat the call, but instead, his body sank a few inches and he took in water. He gagged and instinctively tried to breathe. He sucked in more water and completely filled his lungs. Ponder tried with everything he had to pull himself to the surface again, but he couldn't.

He remembered seeing the wavy sun through the water as he felt himself sinking. He thought how peaceful, and beautiful it was. He began to close his eyes, melting into the warmth which had begun to envelop him. The water, the sun, and the blue-green of the sky began to fade, but not before a beautiful, sparkling hand, reached in and pulled him up, and out of the pond.

Once out, Ponder looked up at the man attached to the hand. He was glowing, and pulsating in a warm, and brilliant, white light. He was wearing a white robe that was tied with a golden rope. He smiled, and Ponder noticed that they were floating upwards.

Ponder looked down on the pond. It was as still as glass, and shimmied in the sunlight. He could see clearly that the head of what he thought was his father, was really only a log. He could even see the body of a small boy laying on the bottom. It didn't alarm him at all.

Ponder felt incredibly peaceful—no, he felt wonderful. He felt as light as a feather, and as expansive as the world. He realized how cramped and uncomfortable he had been before, and he wondered why.

He looked up to the man with him. He wasn't afraid—quite the contrary. He felt jubilation, as if he was reuniting with the oldest, and closest friend, he had ever known. He was also thinking more clearly than he ever had. His thoughts came quickly with nothing drawn out. There was no mental handicap at all. In fact, he felt as if he knew all the answers to every question that had ever been asked.

Ponder looked to the man, and asked him where they were going. He was surprised when the man replied to him without opening his mouth, but instead by just putting the answer in his mind. The man told him they were going to Heaven, and they would be there shortly.

In that very instant, Ponder felt them being pulled through a tunnel. It was iridescent bluish white. He couldn't actually see the walls, but he could feel that they existed. When he looked in the distance, he could see a gloriously bright, white light. It was coming closer. It was the brightest light he had ever seen but it didn't hurt his eyes.

When they arrived at the light, it encased him in a warmth he had never known. It enveloped him in the most perfect love, and peace he had ever felt. Ponder had never been more alive, cherished, beautiful, and perfect.

The young boy looked around. He saw his beloved grandmother, Ruth standing before him. She had died only months earlier. She was beaming and more beautiful than he had ever seen her. She was young—even younger than his own mother—and like the being who had escorted him, she looked at if she was made of a glorious sparkling white light.

The loving being that rescued him from the pond, took his hand and led him toward his grandmother. She bent down to get eye level with him.

She stroked his face, and again, the unimaginable warmth and love permeated every part of him.

"My precious boy, you cannot stay here. You must go back to your mother and father."

Ponder began to cry. "No Granny, I want to stay with you."

Ponder wondered why he wanted to stay, instead of returning to his parents. He loved them so very much, but, he had never felt as good as he had in that moment. He had never felt so sublime. He knew that he was sheer perfection and it wasn't something that he had ever felt while on Earth. It was everything he had ever wanted and more.

As he continued to gaze at his grandmother, the man took him by the hand and began to lead him back toward the tunnel.

"No! I want to stay. Please, please, let me stay here!" he pleaded to them both.

His grandmother smiled and reassured him.

"There will come a day when you will come back and you will stay. But for now Ponder, you have great things to do on Earth. People are relying on you. They need you. You are a great teacher and you will show others how to love unconditionally—how to see beyond the façade and into the soul. You will help change the world because you were there."

The last thing Ponder heard her say was, *"I love you my son and I am always with you."*

And with that, Ponder awoke coughing and choking on the bank of the pond. His father, a complete look of terror on his face, was looking down at him.

"Oh thank you Jesus! Thank you Jesus!" his Pa had cried. "My boy! Thank you Jesus!"

The burly man hugged Ponder to his chest, and sobbed. Ponder didn't know why his Pa was so upset and tried to console him.

"It's okay Pa." He stroked the man's arm. "I's okay."

Ponder sat up and looked down at his heavy body. Then he realized that he couldn't think as clearly, and he began to cry. He shook his head in disbelief. How was he ever going to be able to live on Earth again, after experiencing Heaven?

"It is going to be too hard. I don't think I can do it." He thought to himself.

Then he heard his grandmother's voice.

"I am always with you."

He stopped crying.

Since then, Ponder had heard people describe Heaven. His preacher said it was a wonderful place, full of love and compassion, with no pain and no sorrow. And he knew that was right. But, he also knew it was so much more. It was greater than the human soul could comprehend, and to even try to explain it would be like trying to paint the most beautiful sunset he'd ever seen with a stick in the mud.

Now that his folks were gone, Ponder sometimes found himself feeling guilty, and jealous. He wanted all that glory for his momma and his pa, but he also wanted them to still be with him. If he closed his eyes, he could sometimes smell them. His momma smelled like ivory soap, flour, and nutmeg. His father smelled like hard work.

When he missed them so fiercely that he thought he couldn't go on, he would remember his grandmother's words. Then, he would hum the melody of *You are My Sunshine,* to himself just like his mother had done for so many years. Before he would get to the end, he would trade his humming for singing—his own slow and low base voice, becoming a comfort to him.

>o<

"We just gonna keep sittin here?" an impatient Lorelei asked anyone who would listen. "I wanna go and find Old Pete."

She jumped up and looked down at the rest of them.

Trucker, however, didn't seem as eager to proceed with the adventure. He had laid back in the grass and was watching the stars overhead.

Long John was chewing on a blade of dried grass, while using a stick to poke around in pond mud.

Maybelline was holding Daphney's head in her lap as the tiny woman soundly slept. With her leaf encrusted hands, she pointed to Daphney and shrugged.

"Daphney's sleepin'. Don't think she wants to find Old Pete anymore."

"E'r err erred err," Trucker lazily imparted.

"Me too," Long John agreed. "Imma too tired."

Ponder nodded his head in agreement.

Lorelei couldn't believe what she was hearing.

"What about the mountains? We didn't get to the mountains!" She stomped her foot.

"Er's err erred err errrrerrs," Trucker restated.

"Me too," Long John yawned. "Imma too tired fer mountains too."

Ponder nodded, and Maybelline again pointed to Daphney.

"ARRRRRRRGH," Lorelei screamed. "That's not fair. NOT FAIR! You said we was doin' mountains, and I want mountains!"

"Er." Trucker shook his head. "Err errr."

"No, not gonna," Long John reported.

Trucker got to his feet, and motioned for everyone to follow.

Maybelline gently tapped Daphney on the cheek to wake her up. Daphney wasn't budging, so Maybelline rolled her off her lap and stood up. Daphney woke when her head thumped the ground. She scowled at her friend.

Trucker looked at the rest of them, and then a panicked look came across his stubbly face.

"What's tha matter?" Long John asked him.

Trucker's eyes grew wide.

"Er errerr err Errer Errrrr."

"Yas fergot tha Silly String?" Long John looked alarmed, despite the fact that he wasn't even sure what the Silly String was for.

"Oh no!" Maybelline began to wail, although she did not know its purpose either. She looked down at Ponder who still hadn't made it to his feet. "Trucker forgot the Silly String. What are we gonna do?" Then she looked to Daphney. "What are we gonna do?"

Daphney whimpered.

"What's the Silly String for?" Lorelei, who had already forgotten her anger, had the foresight to question.

Long John looked to Trucker who explained.

Long John's face became ashen and he stepped backwards.

"Ta find our way back?"

"Errr. Er err errer err er er errr er errrr er err er errr." Trucker explained.

"Use it ta make a trail we's could foller?" Long John queried.

Trucker nodded then showed Long John his empty pockets. "Ererr."

Long John looked to Ponder.

"Does ya knows tha way outta hurr?"

"Nope." Ponder shrugged his large shoulders. "I's... don'ts...knows...where...we's...at."

Lorelei, seeing her chance to keep the adventure going, stepped into the middle of them.

"I know where we are, and I know how to get back."

Ponder looked at Long John, who looked to Trucker. Trucker thought it over for a minute.

"Erer. Errr er." He ordered her.

"Kay, show us," Long John repeated.

Lorelei took her place at the front, and led the group west instead of south. They all followed willingly.

Chapter Nineteen

The group trudged through the overgrowth, blindly following Lorelei. She boldly marched ahead as if she had made the trip a thousand times. Her confidence also served to convince the others, that within moments, they would be again entering the wooded area from which they had earlier come.

It was Ponder who first discovered that they were not on the right path home.

"We's…been…walkin'…too…long…to…not…be…in…da…woods. He looked around, trying to assess their location. "I's…thinks…we's…lost."

Everyone stopped and began to look around, searching the landscape for any familiar site.

"I ain't seein' no woods." Long John muttered. "Yas see eny woods?" he asked Trucker.

"Er," Trucker shook his head.

Maybelline began to chastise Lorelei.

"Now look what you did. You got us lost. We're gonna die here!" she dramatically exclaimed.

"NO DIE!" Daphney hunkered to her knees for the third time that night, and began rocking.

"Ain't...gonna...die...Daphney." Ponder tried to reassure her.

"Are," she countered. "Gonna die."

Maybelline chimed in.

"We're gonna die right here cause we don't have no food, we don't have no water, and we don't have no toilet paper."

Both Long John and Ponder looked at the woman. Ponder bit his lip.

"We's...gotta...have...food," he agreed, "and...water, buts,...I...don't...thinks...we's...has...to...have...toilet... paper."

"Yep. He's right." Long John concurred.

Maybelline disagreed.

"Toilet paper is the mostest important thing. Ain't it Daphney?"

Daphney continued rocking herself without responding.

"How else we gonna make our S.O.S. flags?" Maybelline asked the group. "If we don't want to starve, or die of thirst, then we gotta have a rescue flag. Toilet paper flies real good."

"Er err errr." Trucker announced.

"Ya's got food?" Long John turned away from Maybelline, and toward Trucker.

"Errerrs."

"Oh yeah! You got biscuits!" he acknowledged, remembering their latest smuggling trip to the cafeteria.

Trucker pulled the biscuits from his pocket, unwrapped the napkin, and showed them to the onlookers.

"Errr."

He handed them each a piece of bread. He had to poke Daphney to get her attention. Without looking up, she greedily grabbed the crumbling mass, stuck it in her mouth, and then curled back into a rocking ball.

Trucker finished before everyone, and wiped his mouth on the back of his somewhat dingy pajama top. Then he belched so loudly the rest of them jumped.

"Ghosties," Daphney whimpered.

"Nah, jest Trucker burpin', Daphney," Long John replied.

"What...are...we...gonna...do...now?" Ponder addressed Trucker?

Trucker puckered his mouth and tapped his fingers together in thought.

"Er errerr er errr." He pointed to the same direction they had already been heading.

Of all of them, only Ponder seemed to realize that they would be continuing in the wrong direction.

"Ya's...sure...'bout...that?   I's...thinks...that's...where ...we's...was...just...goin'."

"Er errr," Trucker challenged.

"He's sure," Long John shrugged.

The band of Tinsleys fell in line behind Trucker and continued east.

Another ten minutes passed before they came upon a wooded area again.

"Err?" Trucker turned around to his followers and grinned.

"See?" Long John parroted.

"Goody," Daphney clapped her hands. "Home."

As they had before, the Tinsleys entered the darkened woods. This time, Maybelline kept an eye out for any thorny bushes that may grab her already torn night gown.

Ponder watched for any fallen tree trunks, and quickly warned the other when he saw them. Long John swept aside the low hanging grapevines, and the currently dormant Cross Vines and Poison Ivy.

Trucker forged ahead, proud of himself that he was leading his troop home. He became even more self-inflated when they finally stumbled upon Jumper Creek.

"Errr!" he hollered to those behind him, before smugly pointing. "Errrer Errrr."

"Jumper Crick," Long John announced. "Trucker's done found us Jumper Crick."

Everyone began to praise their fearless leader. Trucker's head swelled.

"Ohhhhh," Maybelline looked over into the creek, "It's a pool."

She pointed to a ten foot by ten foot basin that was dammed by a natural stone levy, and was being fed by a small waterfall.

"It ain't deep," she reasoned. "We should swim."

Trucker thought a minute and then gave his approval.

Maybelline was the first to venture in. She dipped a toe and then squealed.

"It's cold. It's really cold."

"Ah ya's jest being a baby," Long John mocked. "Move outta tha way."

He pushed Maybelline aside and took a running step into the water, his body submerging all the way under. When he came up, he gasped, and screamed at the same time.

"Itsa deep! Oh my Gawd... itsa freezin' too!" His eyes bulged out of his head, much to Maybelline's delight.

"I told you Long John. I told you it was cold, and you were bein' mean, and you didn't listen, and that's what you gets for bein' so mean to me!"

Long John pulled himself up the bank as quickly as he could, while water poured from his soggy clothing. He wrapped himself in his own arms, and stood there with his teeth chattering.

"We's gots ta get back to tha home." He shivered. "I's gonna' freeze ta death."

Trucker looked alarmed.

"Err't errrr," he pointed back to the creek.

"Tr-Tr-Trucker says we, we, we's, can't cr-cr-cr-cross." Long John quivered.

"What we gonna do?" Lorelei asked.

The Tinsleys stood looking at each other, waiting for someone to tell them. When no one did, Ponder spoke up.

"We's…just…gonna…have…to…follow…it…'til…we's … finds…a…place…we…can…cross."

"But which way?" Maybelline furrowed her brow as she looked around, trying to figure out which way would lead them home.

The rest turned to Trucker. Unsure too, he finally licked his finger and put it in the air. Everyone watched intently, waiting for his pronouncement.

"Errr err," he pointed north and even further away from their home.

Everyone sighed with relief that their courageous leader was going to save them.

They all fell in line once again and tiredly forged ahead. As they continued, it appeared that the creek had become shallower, but wider. Long John wasn't willing to risk immersing himself into the frigid water again, so even though they could cross in the knee deep current, he wouldn't.

The Tinsleys walked for almost twenty minutes, stumbling and slipping into mud, before Trucker halted them once again and pointed.

"Errr."

"Th-th-th-thur." The still shivering Long John pointed too.

The creek had narrowed considerably and much like the first place they crossed, it consisted mostly of a sand bar encrusted with little pebbles.

"Th-th-thet thur looks g-g-good," Long John agreed. "We's k-k-kin cross hurr."

Not a single one of the Tinsleys were as joyful as they had been on their first trip across Jumper Creek. The cold, weak, and exhausted faction wanted nothing more than to get home and get warm.

Ponder was especially feeling the effects of too little sleep, and too much adventure. Because of his age, he was finding it almost impossible to keep up with his friends. After the rest of them had made it safely to the other side Ponder hadn't even made it to the crossing point. Long John called out to him.

"P-P-P-Ponder, we's over e-e-e-'hurr." Long John waved.

But through the darkness, Ponder found it hard to see them.

"Where's yous at?" he yelled back.

"R-r-r-right hurr. L-l-l-look at tha cr-cr-crick. Y-y-ya's kin cr-cr-cr-cross hurr."

Ponder followed Long John's voice and arrived at the creek. He crossed, but once reunited with his friends, he expressed his frustration.

"I's...awfully...tired." I's...don'ts...thinks...I's...can...go...on."

"Ya's gots ta. We's almost thur; ain't we Trucker?" Long John turned to look down at their leader.

"Er'er ererrr errrr." Trucker lied.

"See, we's almost thur."

Ponder sighed, more weary than he ever remembered being.

"Okay's...I's...gonna...keep...goin'," he relented.

Once they had climbed to the top of the ridge that formed the creek, they all collapsed.

"Want home," Daphney fussed.

"We'll be home in just a few minutes," Lorelei told her. "Remember once we got over the creek, the woods aren't that deep. Before long we'll be at the fields by Old Pete's old house, then our place is just across the street."

"Let's...go...den."

Ponder slowly started to rise. Everyone else was already walking by the time he made it up.

It was a little surprising to Maybelline that they had only walked about ten feet before the woods ended. Maybe they hadn't been as deep as she had thought. No one else seemed to notice, so she saw no reason to mention it.

It wasn't until they had traipsed through the grass for a few yards that Lorelei looked up and announced her surprise.

"Hey, where's the road? Where's Old Pete's old house? Where's our home?" She looked across the seemingly non-ending field in front of them.

The others looked up then too, and began lamenting.

"We's not en tha right place," Long John announced. He turned to Tucker who just shrugged.

As they all tried to figure out what had happened, Ponder caught up with them.

"We's...still...lost."

"Home!" Daphney demanded, as if by her tone she could force them to take her.

Ponder spent several minutes scanning the landscape. Then he nodded. "We's... too... far... north. Sees...it's...gettin'... a...little...lighter...over...dere." He pointed to the east.

Ponder was no stranger to the early morning hours before dawn. When he lived with his ma and pa, he arose by four-thirty each day, so he could have some cornbread and milk to tide him over while he did his chores.

"If...we's...goes...dis...way," he pointed south, "we's... can...get...back...to...da...home."

Not willing to take any more chances finding their way back, they all fell in line behind Ponder. Daphney stayed close to Lorelei, but whined consistently, as if she was a puppy in pain.

"Ponder slow."

Trucker, not wanting to be upstaged, confided in Long John that he bet they were still going the wrong direction.

Maybelline, clearly exhausted, followed the pack wordlessly, while picking at the glue and leaves on her hands.

The filthy entourage tramped through the grass, staggering from time to time, for what seemed like hours. In reality, it had only been a few minutes before Ponder interrupted their zombie like states.

"Dere's…da…ball…field." He pointed to the field that was only a few blocks west of Tinsley's.

Everyone's heads popped up in surprise.

"Hey, how'd we get here?" Maybelline, stopped picking at her hands and looked around.

"Er errr err!" Trucker took credit for bringing the group back to civilization.

"He says he told yas," Long John informed them.

The other members started to protest, but found it too tedious. Instead, knowing where they were, they left the ever slowing Ponder behind, and crossed the ball field on their way home. Within minutes, they would be in their warm and comfy beds.

As soon as they hit North Street, with a newfound burst of energy, Lorelei and Daphney took off running. It wasn't long before Trucker, Long John, and Maybelline, joined them. Ponder however, trailed behind, not having even an ounce of energy left in his body.

By the time he reached North Street, he was lethargically swaying back and forth. Instead of following the others, he continued on to a small white clapboard house on the corner of Division and North. He staggered up on the porch and opened the front door. All was quiet and dark. Directly to the right of the living room, there was a darkened bedroom. All Ponder could think about was sleeping. He laid his weary body down on the feather mattress, and sunk deep into it. Before he exhaled, he was fast asleep.

Trucker opened their secret door and herded the group inside of Tinsley's. He put his finger to his mouth to tell the rest of them to be quiet. Long John was cold to his core. His whole body shook like he was in an earthquake. Trucker sent everyone to their rooms and he and Long John retreated to theirs. Long John—still somewhat dripping—left a trail of water behind them.

"Err errer err errrrrr," Trucker pointed to Long John's wet façade.

Long John fumbled with the buttons on his pajama top, trying to escape his wet clothing.

"I's c-c-c-can't git it unbuttoned," he told Trucker. "M-m-m-my hands are too c-c-c-cold."

Trucker went to his tall friend and began unbuttoning his shirt. Then he helped pull it from around his shoulders and let it drop to the floor. Long John's teeth chattered uncontrollably.

"Er errr er err errr?" Trucker seemed genuinely concerned.

"Yeah, a-a-a-a hot b-b-b-bath en I'd be g-g-g-good."

"Errr errr er er errr er err."

Trucker told Long John to wait, as he fixed a bath. Before he left the room to enter the bathroom, Trucker grabbed the bedspread from his bed, and wrapped it around his freezing friend.

Long John heard the water run, and became worried that an aide might hear it too. With his foot, he pushed the shirt on the floor toward the door. When he reached it, he closed the door and tucked it beneath to mute any sound that might escape their room.

Trucker went to the bathroom door to inform Long John that his bath was ready.

Long John shuffled to the bathroom, teeth still chattering. He handed the bedspread back to Trucker, took off his wet pajama bottoms and slowly eased into the steaming water. At first it felt like a million needles pricking his already tortured skin, but as soon as his flesh grew accustomed to the temperature change, Long John sank as far down as his long frame would let him and he surrendered to the warm comfort.

"Itsa like a hug from my granny." He turned to Trucker. "Think ya Trucker."

Trucker saw the intense appreciation in Long John's eyes, and it took him aback. There had never been anyone in his life who had looked at him like his friend just had. It was then he realized that Long John truly loved him.

"Er errerrr," Trucker shyly replied, and stepped out of the bathroom to let his best friend—no, his brother—thaw.

Chapter Twenty

Trucker and Long John both awoke at the same time. It only took them a moment to orient themselves to the commotion taking place in the hall. They jumped out of their beds and ran to their door, Long John reaching it first and flinging it open.

At the nurses' station stood Ponder and Lester, the police officer. Lester was making quite a scene.

"Ya can't just let 'em' run all over town in the middle of the night," he admonished Margie the charge nurse. "One of 'em is gonna get hurt or worse, they're gonna hurt someone else!"

Margie was nodding her head in agreement.

"I understand Lester. I don't know how he got out of here."

She turned accusingly toward Ponder.

"How'd you get outta here Ponder?"

Ponder starred at her without reply, and Margie returned her gaze to Lester.

"I promise you Lester, it won't happen again," she apologized.

"You are right 'bout that," Lester slapped the counter of the nurses' station. "Cuz there have been way too many problems with your Tinsleys lately, and townsfolks are getting mighty tired of it."

Margie's eyes grew wide. "What do you mean?"

"You know what I'm talking about Margie." Lester took out a grimy handkerchief and wiped his sweaty forehead. "Last month ya had that one that broke out the drugstore window so he could steal a smoking pipe."

"Errrerr," Trucker whispered.

"Yep, Milton," Long John repeated, talking about a rather bashful yet sometimes aggressive resident.

Margie tried to defend him.

"Now Lester you know that he wasn't trying to steal from Stephen's Drug. It was Sunday. They were closed. He left money in the window.

"Er errr errer." Trucker reasoned.

"He did leave money," Long John agreed.

Lester raised an eyebrow, but continued his tirade.

"Last year ya had that little dumpy one that trashed Mrs. Doodle's place."

Knowing Lester was talking about Trucker, Long John looked to his friend. Trucker growled under his breath, angry at being called little and dumpy.

"And now ya got 'em breakin' into people's houses, and putting themselves to bed. This un almost scared Coach Wren, and his poor wife, half to death. Good Lord in high heaven Margie, what's next—streakin' down Main Street?"

Lester's face had gotten redder by the moment.

Margie sighed, having no answer, because she knew it was a distinct possibility. In fact Emmalean Nader had broken into the swimming pool for a midnight skinny dip about five years earlier. Margie was glad that Lester hadn't remembered that incident.

"It's gonna stop now. I've already put in a call to Mr. Tinsley," Lester reported. "There are to be no more Tinsleys out in town on their own. If ya'll are gonna let 'em out, ya have to supervise them."

Margie, Ponder, Long John, and Trucker, all gasped at the same time. Margie spotted the two loiterers and pointed at them.

"You two come here!"

Long John and Trucker began to back into their room.

"Oh no you don't!" she yelled at them. "You git your ornery butts back here right now."

Long John grabbed Trucker by the arm, and both of them reluctantly approached their commander in chief.

Margie pointed to Ponder.

"I know you two had a part in this. You better start talking."

"Er err't errr errr err errrr'n errrr." Trucker put up his hands innocently.

"He don't know what yer talkin' 'bout," Long John told her.

"Oh but *you* do, don't you Long John?" Margie eyed him hard.

"No ma'am," Long John lowered his guilty head.

"Ponder, are you going to tell me what happened, or am I going to have to discipline all of you?"

"I's...don't...know...Miss...Margie," Ponder lied, then bit his lip. "Maybe's... I's...wasa...sleepwalkin'."

"How'd you get out of here?" The nurse put her hands on her hips, not believing a word Ponder said.

A group of Tinsleys had now gathered around the station, including Lorelei, Daphney, and Maybelline. The three huddled together in fear.

"We gonna get caught," Maybelline whispered to Lorelei.

Daphney looked up at her in terror. Lorelei pulled her back behind the crowd to admonish her.

"Don't ya dare say a thing, Daphney. If we don't say nothin' then we ain't gonna get caught."

Daphney nodded.

Lester chimed in with Margie's interrogation.

"You boys have done it now, cuz ya ain't gonna be able to go anywhere on your own, including into town."

The entire assembly of Tinsleys began to protest, and Margie, sensing a riot, tried to placate them.

"Now, now, Lester, that's a little extreme don't you think?"

The Tinsleys waited with baited breathe to hear Lester's response.

"No I do not." He turned to the gatherers. "If ya'll can't behave yourselves any better than this, then it's how it's gonna be."

Margie tried to fight for the inhabitants and play on Lester's sympathy.

"Lester," she smiled sweetly at the officer, "there's no way we can take our residents into town and supervise them. We just don't have the manpower. It would be a shame to keep them locked up here all the time. They get bored, and there's nothing for them to do here. You wouldn't want to have to live like that would you?"

"That ain't my problem Margie. My problem is all the townsfolks who are callin' me all the time complainin' bout these here residents." Lester made quotation signs around the word residents.

"There's not a week that goes by that I ain't getting' a call 'bout this one." He pointed to Trucker. "He's a nuisance, always gettin' in the back of people's trucks, and refusing to get out."

Trucker growled at Lester and he took a step backwards.

"Ya see what I mean? They're unpredictable at best, and like I said, they're gonna hurt someone at worst."

Lester turned and looked around at the rest of the Tinsleys.

"I've made up my mind. From now on, none of ya better go off on yer own, or I'm gonna arrest ya and put ya in Lula. And mark my words, you don't want to get thrown in Lula," (which unbeknownst to anyone, is what Lester called the jail).

A unanimous "Awwww," of disapproval went out from the crowd. Lester ignored it and turned to go. Before he reached the door he turned back. He pointed to the still assembled Tinsleys.

"I mean it now. Don't ya test me."

The mass booed and hissed him all the way out the door.

Once Lester had exited the building, the disgruntled Tinsleys turned on their charge nurse.

"You gotta fix this!" Milton cried. "I has to go inta town. I love town. I can't live without town!"

"Yeah!" everyone else agreed.

"Calm down, calm down." Margie patted the air around her. "I'll talk to Mr. Tinsley and see if he can't talk some sense into Lester, but in the meantime, you all stay put," she ordered.

Grumbling and groaning ensued as the group split up and went their own ways—all except the six Tinsleys who were responsible for the debacle.

"Errr er err errr," Trucker ordered.

"Come ta our room," Long John repeated.

When the trouble makers reassembled, Ponder was the first to speak.

"Imma...sorry." He hung his head in shame. "I's... neber...meant...to...git...us...in...trouble.

I's…just…neber…
been…dat…tired…in…ma…whole…life."

"It ain't yer fault." Long John shook his head. "We's all snucked out, not jest you."

Maybelline and Lorelei agreed and when Daphney saw them, she nodded her head too.

"Er errer errr er err err err ererrr," Trucker told them.

"We gonna have ta lay low fer awhile," Long John told them.

Trucker leaned in and whispered to Long John. He turned to the others.

"We kin still go out at night cuz theys don't know 'bout our door."

"Yeah!" Lorelei exclaimed. "Even if we can't go out to town in the day, we can still go at night."

Then she hesitated, and sighed.

"Probably won't be as much fun."

Maybelline lightened the assumption.

"At least we won't be stuck here all the time."

The rest of them agreed with her.

As the group began to leave, Long John gave them a final warning.

"Don't nobody tell nobody 'bout last night. Iffin we keep its ta ourselves, thur never gonna find us out."

"Errrr," Trucker chimed in.

"Shhhh," Long John put his finger to his mouth. "Quiet."

Chapter Twenty-One

The following morning, Nurse Margie called all Tinsleys to a meeting in the game room. When everyone was assembled, she informed them of her conversation with Mr. Tinsley.

"I've got some really good news for ya'll." She smiled. "Mr. Tinsley is getting us a small bus so that we can take you into town one day a week."

Margie looked around the room to see if the residents were buying her "good news" façade. They weren't.

"NOOOOOOO!" yelled someone in the back of the room.

"We wanna go on our own!" Lorelei demanded.

"Yeah and I wanna go more than once a week!" Milton stood up and shoved his fist into the air. "I wanna go every day!"

It wasn't lost on Margie, that in the past, Milton usually only went to town once a week.

The elderly residents, who never went into town at all, remained quiet, watching the drama unfold. The temporary lull was interrupted by Stubby who came to the front of the room to voice his displeasure. He stood there for a moment swaying back and forth. Then, before expressing his sentiments, he lifted his shirt and showed the crowd his pasty belly.

"That ain't fair," he softly said, then returned to his chair and sat down.

"Thank you for your opinion Stubby," Margie placated him.

Trucker looked over at him and glared.

"Listen here," Margie sighed. "We don't have a choice in this. Mr. Tinsley feels like if we keep up the status quo, he is going to get sued."

"Who's Sue?" someone asked.

"Who's Quo?" asked another.

The nurse ignored them.

"Never mind about that. Here's the bottom line. You are still going to get to go to town. If your family or friends want to take you, you can go at any time. If not, we go once a week—maybe twice if you're really good—and the best part is you're going to get to ride a bus!"

Daphney was the only one of the sneaking Tinsleys who seemed somewhat excited about the idea.

"Bus," she giggled.

Nurse Margie waited for the continued outcry of protests, but the room had gone silent. It seemed as if the tenants had run out of ammunition.

"Okay then," she smiled, happy that they had avoided total mayhem, "the first trip into town will be Thursday."

She looked around the now quiet room, assessing if it was still safe to continue. All eyes were on her, and mouths remained closed.

"We will go at 11:00 a.m.; that way if you want to have lunch there you can. Meeting is over."

The room quickly cleared, but heads were still low.

>o<

The night-time gang didn't lay low very long before they decided to exit Tinsley's for greater adventures. They had all gone into town that first Thursday, and they did indeed enjoy riding the bus. Daphney especially, who jumped up and down on her seat, bobbing the entire five minute trip. Trucker, Long John, and Ponder, made sure to have lunch at the Eater Upper while the girls spent their time shopping.

The following day however, Trucker, was not a happy camper. While Ponder napped in the bus, he and Long John went to Stephen's Drug for Double Bubble. They each bought one piece of gum, forgetting that they couldn't get more the next day.

On Friday—when Trucker got a gum hankering, and told Long John he was ready to go get some—only then did he realize that he had no way to get it. He erred his displeasure loudly, while throwing a massive fit. Long John tried to smooth things over.

"Next time we's goes ta tha drugstore, we's gonna git seven pieces each. Thet way, we'lls have enough ta last us 'til we's gets ta go again."

Trucker agreed, but unhappily.

"Errr er errerr er err errr?" he asked his friend.

240

"I's guess we's jest gonna have ta wait."

Trucker growled, then whimpered. It upset Long John horribly.

"Maybe we's kin sneak out tanight en git some," he reasoned.

"Er'll er errrrr." Trucker responded.

"Yeah, thur gonna be closed, but maybe thu'll ferget ta lock tha back doors."

Truckers eyes became wide and bright. "Errr." He smiled. "Errr!"

That night the group gathered as they always had, and headed for town. When they got there, they checked the streets to make sure they were empty. Lester's police car was parked in front of city hall, so they snuck up to the window to peer inside.

Lester was nowhere to be seen, but a bleach blonde young girl sat inside at a dimly lit, small desk. She smacked on some gum (making Trucker jealous), and worked on a crossword puzzle. She twirled her hair around her fingers.

Just as the group turned to leave, they heard a squawking voice come from a black box like contraption with a long microphone.

"Konawa PD, this is Seminole PD, over."

The girl pulled it in front of her, pushed a square button on its base, and spoke into the microphone.

"This is Konawa PD, over."

"Whatcha doin' girl?" a lively, and less formal voice than before, responded.

"I'm bored," the blonde girl whined. "Nothing ever happens here."

"I hear ya," the other voice responded.

"Yeah but at least you get calls at night. I haven't had a single one since I got this job six months ago, over."

"Yeah, I guess I would rather be busy than bored," the other voice relented.

"Yeah. Anything going on with you?"

"Nope, pretty quiet tonight. That's why I'm hollering at you," the voice laughed. "But I guess I better get off here in case one of the guys needs me."

"Okay," the girl sighed. "Have a good one."

"You too, over."

The Tinsleys looked at each other. Trucker shrugged and then motioned for his entourage to follow him. They snuck away from the police station, and crossed the street at a diagonal, landing in front of Stephen's Drug. Trucker looked around before sneaking up to the door to see if it might be unlocked. It wasn't. Trucker growled and turned to Long John. He looked incredibly, and pitifully sad.

"Don't cha worry," Long John placated his friend. "Let's go en check tha back."

Trucker nodded, still looking worried, but flagged his minions to follow. They walked back down the street, and turned the corner. They snuck beside the car wash and made it to the alley. Then, they headed back up the little dirt and gravel road behind the buildings.

About half way up, Trucker gestured for everyone to stop.

"Errrr err er er?" he asked.

"I don't rightly knows which one its is," Long John answered. "Thur's no signs."

Trucker looked at the rest of the group, who blankly returned his stare.

"Err errr?"

"He wants ta know iffin yous knows?"

Heads shook back and forth in unison.

"Kay, we's gonna try 'em all," Long John finally decided.

Trucker walked to the metal door of the building where they had stopped. He turned the knob, but it was locked. He hmphed.

Long John had already moved on to the second one. It was boarded up, so he knew there was no getting in. They tried several more before stopping at two large and rusted, fifty gallon oil drums at the road's edge. The barrels were used as trash cans. Ponder pointed to them.

"Dis…here…is…da…drugstore."

"Howda yas know?" Long John asked.

"Cause…dere's…a...bunch…of…dose…pill…bottles…in…it," he concluded.

Trucker, in jubilation, slapped Ponder on the back.

"Err er," he instructed Long John, who walked to the large gray door, and tried to open it.

The handle turned, and Maybelline gasped. Daphney clapped.

When the handle had turned as far as it could, Long John pushed to open the door. It wouldn't budge, so he tried harder. Still, it wouldn't open.

"Awwww, dang! It's stuck," Lorelei pronounced.

Trucker let out a frustrated little shriek, and stomped the ground trying to kill it. Long John did what Long John always did, and tried to cool him off.

"Yas know, we kin try Ralph's."

Trucker stopped stomping, and looked up at him.

"Err."

The six Tinsleys continued up the alleyway. They stopped at Ralph's, which was easy to spot, because it had a water pump with a handle out back. It was also the only store that let customers come in from the back through its double wooden doors. Both Trucker and Long John had done it many times before.

Trucker turned to the rest.

"E'r errer' err errr. Errr errr.

"He's tryin' tha door. Wait here.

As if he owned the place, Trucker boldly walked to the door and grabbed its metal barn door handle. He pulled as hard as his fleshy little body would allow. The door careened open and threw him off balance, onto his butt.

The group thought they were about to witness yet another Trucker fit, but when he looked up at them, he had huge grin on his face.

"Er's erer!"

"Itsa open alright," Long John declared. "Let's go."

He bent over to help his friend up, then he ushered Trucker in with a sweep of his hand. Trucker ran inside the darkened building.

Only a moment later, the rest of the group heard a skidding thunk, followed by a strand of Trucker style cussing.

The pudgy Tinsley had forgotten about the uneven cement ramp at the door. He gathered himself, and then pushed through a second set of swinging doors that separated the back entrance from the meat counter and the rest of the store.

Once inside the shadowy store, Trucker turned to his followers, and warned them.

"Err't errr er errrrr er err't errrr erer errren'"

Long John put his finger to his lips.

"Don't make no noise en don't crash inta nothin'.

Trucker headed toward the front of the store, and the candy area which was located near the front windows. He squinted in the dark, trying to locate his prize. He found it on the second shelf.

"Errerr!" he turned to show Long John.

"Double Bubble," Long John agreed.

Trucker counted out fourteen pieces for himself, and his best friend. He left a quarter, and a nickel on the counter behind him.

Ponder announced that he might like to get an apple while they were there. He told the others to wait while he made his way to the produce section on the far north wall. In a few moments, Ponder returned with a big red apple. He held it for the others to see.

"Red... Delicious. Ma...favorite."

"Ya gonna leave some money for it?" Maybelline asked.

"I's...already...did." Ponder took a large bite of the fruit he held, then swallowed it. "I's...left...it...with...da... rest...of...da...apples."

"Err's er errr," Trucker ordered.

"He says, let's go," Long John imparted.

The little group of Tinsleys slowly made their way out of Ralph's and closed the door behind them.

ACKNOWLEDGEMENTS

As an author, it is fortunate to find people you trust implicitly with your work. I have been that lucky, from almost the beginning.

I wish to thank my first readers, who also serve as editors, Carol Cervi McCurdy and Barbara DePrater Gregory. I appreciate the sacrifices these woman make, by taking time out of their own lives to help me. They are, and have, been an invaluable asset.

Next, I want to again thank my daughter, Brealyn Brashier Wren, who is the incredible talent behind the covers of this series. She never fails to see my vision and bring it to life. Her work is always better than I could have even imagined.

And to you, dear reader, your continued support of this series means the world. Thank you.

ABOUT THE AUTHOR

SD Shelton is the award-winning, and best-selling author, of the memoir *Me, the Crazy Woman, and Breast Cancer.* She is also the author of The Drugstore Series and is a multi-award-winning, former broadcast, and print journalist.

SD first knew she wanted to write books when she was in sixth grade. A spark ignited in her that never went out after reading, *Are You There God? It's Me, Margaret* by Judy Blume. She actually even tried to write a book then, but after only a few pages, it became apparent that her eleven-year-old self didn't have a lot to say.

She did have the good sense to become a journalist, which allowed her to indulge in her love of writing, and story-telling. When she had to confront two battles with breast cancer, she knew she finally had her own story worth telling.

Me, the Crazy Woman, and Breast Cancer, was released in 2009 with great support and acclaim and she was named "Oklahoma's Best Author" by the *Oklahoma Gazette,* the state's largest and most influential, arts and entertainment publication. It still remains a best-seller on Amazon for books about breast cancer.

SD lives in Oklahoma, with her two barky, and rambunctious Miniature Schnauzers. Walter Roux, and Harvard Winslow (also known as Wally and Harvey), were born in Konawa, and have their own following on Facebook. Connect with them @TheBiteyBabies.

The Tinsleys is the fifth book of eight, in The Drugstore Series. Watch for the sixth installment, *The Fight for Bengal Billy*.

Connect with SD on Facebook @SDSheltonBooks or on Twitter @StacyDShelton.